# Lance

## The Early Journals of Will Barnett 2

by
Ronald L. Donaghe

A Two Brothers Press Book

Two Brothers Press

For information address:
PO Box 264
Columbus, MS 39703
www.twobrotherspress.biz

# Dedication

Reflect upon the truth, herein, despite the claim that this is a purely fictitious work, there are those youth in every school, large or small, in urban areas or in rural places, who suffer the stigma of being different, who love in the shadows, yet present themselves differently in the light—or suffer the consequences. It is not that they love less or less genuinely, only differently. They should not be hurt as a consequence.

# Contents

# Part One
# Found Out

## One
## I Meet Will Barnett
## November 2001

Will Barnett suggested in his e-mail that we meet in Kranberry's restaurant in Lordsburg, New Mexico. Oddly enough, that is where I first read his journal about his Uncle Sean Martin, much of it written in a Big Chief Tablet around 1969.

I had a good idea how Will Barnett would look, since he had described both himself and his Uncle Sean as having blond hair and blue eyes, and himself as being big for his age at fourteen. He was now forty-six, so I had no idea what the intervening years had done to him—until I saw the rather striking man who stood just inside the doorway of the restaurant, looking around. I knew it was him. Although a cap covered most of his hair, in the slanting sunlight of that late November afternoon making its way into the building, I saw blond strands. I wasn't prepared, however, for what had to be his six-foot-three (or four) inches, nor his well-muscled appearance. The light just seemed to gather around him, and almost everyone in the restaurant turned to look. Even though he was wearing the typical southwestern costume of boots, Wranglers, long-sleeved western cut shirt of solid green, and cap with the bill turned to the front, he somehow looked as though he belonged in a classier place. In comparison, the rest of us in the restaurant, in our own casual clothing, looked as if we belonged here—like truckers looking for a quick chicken-fried steak, or farmers and ranchers in for a cup of coffee. I am only seven years older than Will, but there's nothing about me that takes even a month off my fifty-three years. Nor am I hard-bodied. My muscles don't stay toned when I live behind a desk and have only my yard work.

I waved as he looked around the restaurant before moving out of the light of the all-glass door. He saw me and nodded. As he strode toward me, I got up and stuck out my hand.

He presented me with a toothy smile and gripped my hand in an iron fist. "So, you're the guy who stole my work."

I grinned back, but didn't drop my eyes. "No. I'm the guy who rescued it from the rats."

He laughed and I was relieved. I noticed that he was carrying a copy of the book. "You want me to autograph that?" I asked, as I sat back down and nodded at an empty chair.

He pulled the chair away from the table and sat down, removing the cap and tossing it and the book onto the table next to a set-up of napkin-wrapped utensils. "Hell yeah, I want it autographed." Then he frowned through his grin. "And next time, I want my name in print on the cover and not just chicken scratched on it. You did say, didn't you, that you were sure my readers would like to hear from me, again?"

I have to confess, I didn't know until that moment how he really felt about my publishing his journals from so long ago, without getting his permission. We had e-mailed back and forth a couple of times, once he had discovered that his story had been published; but he wouldn't tell me what he thought, only that he liked the way the book turned out and that it was embarrassing to know other people were reading his story. I was glad he spoke of a "next time." It felt odd, however, to be meeting him in the flesh. As I had edited his writing and smoothed out some of the words from his journals, he had taken on the dimensions of one of my characters, rather than a real person.

It didn't take long for a waitress to interrupt our conversation. She was wearing a pink skirt and white blouse and looking rather stunned as she took in the sight of Will Barnett. She had already brought me coffee and iced water, and I had told her I wouldn't order until the other party got here. Now, I became invisible as she hovered next to him, smiling and giving him all the attention she would give George Strait or Garth Brooks, if they had just happened by. I felt the same way she did, in fact—struck by his beauty and what I call masculine grace. Something, anyway, that must come from a lifetime of being stared at and, no doubt, pursued as the good-looking man he was. Rather than being conceited about his looks, however, he met people with an easy-going grace.

He treated the waitress kindly and ordered a salad and steak. "But hold that dressing, darlin', let the steak bleed a little, and I'll have a glass of your house red."

Then she turned reluctantly away from him, pen poised above the order pad. "And what'll you have?"

"Relleno plate—dry. Rice and beans," I said.

When she was gone, a thousand questions presented themselves to me as I watched him settle down.

Will spoke first: "Your e-mail said you have a husband?" I noticed that he didn't lower his voice, apparently not caring who might hear, and I liked that. The intervening years hadn't diminished what I had discovered was his self-confidence. I think it began early, like the time he had stared down Dick Lamb in the locker room at the high school in Animas when Dick asked Will if he was a faggot for his uncle. How Will handled it with humor, without admission—or denial—seems to have set the tone for the levelheaded way he treats the issue now. He doesn't lower his voice. He doesn't appear to worry who might overhear.

"Yes. I told you about Cliff, didn't I?" I said. "We've been together for almost ten years. You didn't mention anyone in your e-mail," I reminded him. "I was wondering if you and Lance might still be together. That would be remarkable."

He grinned at me, then, his eyes twinkling. "I deliberately didn't tell you. If you're going to present my story, I want to keep it chronological. No sense in jumping too far ahead. You think?"

All I could say, just then, was "you've been thinking about this for a while, haven't you?"

"Ever since I happened onto my book."

"Is that why you wouldn't tell me what you thought about your story being published?"

He nodded. "I'll tell you it was hard, reading that first part. Made me out to be a horny little devil, didn't it?"

I just laughed. "You weren't unique in that," I said. "What fourteen year-old boy isn't?"

He smiled back. "I guess you're right, though it was strange having my kid-self exposed like that."

"Can you at least tell me a little about your uncle?"

This time he laughed. "Look. I brought a whole passel of notebooks with me. If you don't find what you're looking for in there, give me a call, and I'll tell you everything you want to know."

Whatever the years had wrought on his life, Will Barnett had come this far with a sense of humor and that air of self-confidence and masculine grace. Realizing I wasn't going to get any details that afternoon about his "story," I tried a simpler question.

"How long has it been since you've seen Hachita? After reading about your uncle's dog tags and how you cherished them, I have to admit I'm curious as to why you left them in the barn."

There was something in his face, just then, that made my heart pound, something that looked like intense sadness. As he would have said of his Uncle Sean, when Will smiled, his beauty shone through like the sun behind a rain cloud. "I never intended to leave any of that stuff there. But the way things went down, we were all a little rushed in the end. I haven't been back here since 1974. You do have them, don't you? Uncle Sean's tags?"

I'd left my briefcase on the floor. It was my turn to smile at him. "I brought everything I found in the barn," I said, picking up the briefcase. I opened it on the empty chair next to me and pulled out the Big Chief Tablet, the letter from Sean, and the spiral notebook and set them on the table. Then I picked up the tags, watching his face as I did so. Tears shone in his eyes, and when I placed them in his outstretched hand, without hesitation, he put the chain around his neck and slipped them under his shirt.

"And do I get my other property back?" he asked, nodding at the tablet and spiral notebook.

"Of course you do. I'm just glad they weren't destroyed."

He pulled the Big Chief toward him on the table, then picked it up and flipped through the pages with a thumb and forefinger, bringing it to his nose and taking a breath. Again, there were tears in his eyes. Then he picked up his Uncle Sean's letter, folded it gently and placed it in his shirt pocket. "This sure brings back memories, as if it were just yesterday. Sean is going to be surprised."

At that last statement, I realized two things. His uncle was still alive (though I had no reason to believe otherwise, since he was only a year older than me), and Will hadn't called him "Uncle," which implied a familiarity of equals, rather than an older family member. But I didn't call him on that; I didn't want him to know he'd slipped up and unintentionally given me information.

When our order came, we tended to eat in silence as two strangers might, even though I felt as if I knew him as intimately as I knew any of the characters from my novels. But there was no denying that he was real as I watched him enthusiastically dig into his rare steak. His hands were young looking and I doubted he'd spent his adulthood as a common laborer. The skin was too smooth and not as tanned as it might be if he had worked outdoors a great deal.

His southwestern clothing was a clue that he had not become a denizen of say, San Francisco, or some other cosmopolitan city—unless of course he was merely dressing the part for our meeting to fit in. People here almost uniformly wear denim and boots and caps, and in many cases, even if they're "dressing up" it means they'll change into a new pair of Wranglers or Levi's. His clothing was new, but his cap wasn't, though it wasn't sweat stained, either.

As we ate, the light outdoors began to fade into gold and the lights inside the restaurant seemed to grow brighter.

We both declined the dessert the waitress offered. But we stayed on to talk and become more acquainted. He switched from wine to coffee as we sat there and, after he had read passages from his long-time-ago writing, he collected them on his side of the table and slid the book toward me.

"I'd be pleased if you'd autograph this, now," he said.

"Anything in particular you'd like me to inscribe?" I asked, as I pulled a pen from my shirt pocket.

He grinned at me over the cup he held to his lips. I saw that he was wearing a wedding band, and I figured he had fulfilled one of his dreams.

He caught me glancing at it. "Yeah. Make it to Will Barnett and his husband."

"And what is your husband's name?" I asked, hoping he might slip up again.

He laughed and winked. "I call him 'honey,' but I better not catch you calling him that."

Not once had he consciously lowered his voice. Even though the restaurant was relatively empty and the nearest customers were two tables away, he had the kind of voice that carried. I glanced left and right and did note that some people had turned their heads in our direction.

"'Husband' it is, then," I said, and wrote that and something else on the dedication page, signed my name, and handed it back.

He read the inscription and smiled at me for a moment, catching my eyes with his own. If anything, they were a deeper, purer blue than the way he described his Uncle Sean's, and I thought of the brilliant hazel green of my partner Cliff's eyes. I've always been a sucker for men with beautiful eyes, and his were no different. For forty-six, his face was still smooth, and like me, I felt that his husband was probably a lucky man. Nothing in Will's demeanor hinted that he had changed from the deeply caring person he had been as a teen, and I was itching to get my hands on the rest of his story.

We chit-chatted for a little while, then parted, agreeing to stay in touch by e-mail. I was a little surprised that, when we walked outdoors and went to his vehicle, it was a Dodge pickup truck, and I wondered if I might have been wrong that he hadn't been a man who worked outdoors after all. Further, if he had driven from a city someplace, it would almost necessarily have been nearby, say El Paso, Phoenix, or Albuquerque; otherwise, I figured he'd be driving a rental car. But I didn't want to ask. He wouldn't have told me, anyway.

He had packed his journals into two Xerox printer-paper boxes, neatly labeled with the sequence of years. As he loaded them into the cab of my own pickup, I said, "At least I know you never quit writing."

We shook hands. "Sometimes, keeping a journal has been about the only thing that has kept me sane."

"I know what you mean," I said. And with that, we said good-bye. I had a two-hour drive ahead of me to get back to Las Cruces. I thought about staying in the parking lot to see which direction he headed, but changed my mind. He had said my questions would be answered in his journals. Now it was up to me to do the work to bring another portion of his story to life.

Just as I did in Will Barnett's first set of journals, which I entitled Uncle Sean, I will attempt to divide his writing into parts and chapters in a way that makes sense to me. When it feels appropriate, I will also give names to those parts, so that readers get a sense of the flow and significant events in "The Continuing Journals of Will Barnett."

# Two
# Lance and Me
# And How People Found Out

It's just now dawn and tender light has begun to enter our bedroom without the glare, here on the northwest side of the house. I'm propped up against the headboard with my pillow tucked beneath the small of my back. I've shoved the sheet off and have this spiral notebook resting on my thighs. It's a new one and these are the first words I've written. Lance is still asleep on his stomach, close to me. With the sheet just covering his butt, I can see the way the light glows softly on his back and shoulders, the way it caresses his cheek and causes his hair to glow against the pillow. His long lashes and lips are still in the shadow of the crook of his arm, face turned toward me.

In a little while I have to wake him, as it's a school day, and we have to drive close to fifty miles to school, there in Animas. But for now I want to get caught up writing down stuff that's happened in the last few weeks, now that school's going on. It's almost October and things are going pretty well—except for two things that have happened lately.

One was with my sister Rita's boyfriend, Rick Zumwalt, which led to the other thing that happened yesterday, which was a Sunday. I haven't told anybody about this second thing—not Mama, not Lance, not even May. I don't want to say anything to

Mama, because Margie Collins and Mama are close friends, and Mrs. Collins has really been good to the girls. I haven't told May, my older sister, because she's the kind that gets mad quick, and does something about it, and I don't think that's a good idea right now. It would probably only make things worse, anyway. I haven't even told Lance, yet, but he needs to know that people are onto us being boyfriends—or at least there's talk about it. Right now it's only talk and not proof, but Mrs. Collins was testing me when she pulled what she did, and now she's probably mad or at least red-faced.

I'm a little red-faced, too, even thinking about it. It's exactly the kind of thing Uncle Sean never would do with me, even though I thought I was ready for it. He was too honorable and told me it would be wrong for an adult to make love to a kid. And though I'm not really a kid anymore, since I turned eighteen, already, I'm still in high school. He wouldn't do it with me, also, because he's my uncle. So, it's even worse to me that Mrs. Collins came onto me like she did, because she's Mama's age. She may not be a relative, but she's old enough to be my mother.

I knew she was interested in me (though I never dreamed she would take it any further), like the day she came over to take Trinket off to her house to spend the night with her daughter Julie. That was the day Daddy was put in the hospital over in Deming—just the day before he died. We were waiting on Trinket to get her stuff together when Mrs. Collins came up to me real close by the door and wrapped her fingers around my upper arm, close enough I could smell her perfume and her sweat. I felt uneasy for her to be so close, because I'd seen the way her eyes bugged out of her head one time when she came to visit and Uncle Sean was sitting in the kitchen without a shirt on. She couldn't take her eyes off him. That's how she began to look at me as I got a little older.

She's married, too, and besides her daughter Julie, she has an older daughter who's already off somewhere going to college, or married, or working. I've never paid enough attention to find out. She's not a bad looking woman, but in comparison to the way Mama dresses, which looks pretty normal to me, Mrs. Collins tries to dress like a high school girl with all her makeup and jewelry, and her short skirts and sweaters that show off her boobs underneath—only she doesn't have all that much to show. She's at least fifty, like Mama. If I were interested in women, I might think Mrs. Collins was kind of pretty. She's probably got a good figure for an old woman. Better than Mama's probably, only I'm just not interested. Besides, everybody knows she hangs out with other men at the bars when her husband Nick is off on business. He's away a lot, though they own a ranch down the road from here, across the highway. Maybe they're rich, though I don't know what that means. Ranchers like the Collins and the Hills run most of the county. Anyway, Mrs. Collins has black hair right now, but I think it was blonde when Daddy died. That was only two months ago.

So yesterday, Lance and May were working in the barn. It's coming up on harvest, and they were cleaning tools and straightening the barn for the grain we'll store there. I headed over to Animas to contact Mr. Trujillo about hiring him this year to harvest the grain with his combine. Daddy always hired him. He thought Mr. Trujillo was a snake in the grass but said he had no choice. As it's coming near October, it was a beautiful day. The air was nippy, but I drove with my window down, and the clean desert air felt good as it dried the sweat on my neck and in my hair. I had been up early for a Sunday and had already been working in the barn before Lance and May showed up. So I was already dirty and probably had grease on my T-shirt.

But that's just the way it is when you have to work all the time. I didn't change clothes as I headed for Animas. Our farm is twenty miles south of Hachita, and from there it's another thirty miles west to Animas. But I enjoyed the drive, and by the time I'd talked to Mr. Trujillo, I went over to the gin where they sell burlap sacks, because this year I'm going to sack up the grain right off the combine and not sell it to Old Man Hill like Daddy used to. Hill has a grain silo, and he buys our grain in bulk, then sacks it up and sells it out himself, and I'm hoping to cut him out, because I need to get as much as I can for the grain, since we don't raise cotton anymore.

Anyway, Mr. Trujillo said he was sorry about Daddy, and I thanked him. Then, I said I'd come to ask him to harvest the grain. He said he would but that he was going to have to charge more with the diesel prices like they were, which is another reason I want to cut out Mr. Hill as the middleman.

So with a little time on my hands before I had to head home, I drove on over to Cotton City, about ten miles north of Animas. It's a nice drive and I wanted to see the fields of cotton, the white fluff against the close-in Peloncillo Mountains that border the west side of the valley, and the clear blue of the sky above it. There's something about a fall sky in the desert that hints at the peace of winter to come, and not just the end of the growing season when plants are dying. Other than summer, fall is my favorite time of the year.

So anyway, I went into the Cotton City Market and bought myself a RC Cola, which I downed in one long swallow and was just getting into my pickup when Mrs. Collins caught my upper arm, wrapping those fingers with their long red nails around it. I almost jerked my arm free, because I didn't recognize her at first with the black hair and red cat-eye sunglasses. I noticed how fake the hair color was, especially out in the sunlight, but I told her how nice it looked.

She got this real funny look on her face. "I was wondering if you even noticed things like that," she said, removing her sunglasses and releasing my arm, for which I was relieved. And I asked her what she meant, because I sure had no idea. I thought I was giving her a compliment and was being polite.

"Just things I've heard," she said, messing with her hair, now that I'd brought it up. She looked around the parking lot as cars pulled away and others drove in, so I thought we were through talking.

"Well, nice seeing you," I said, trying to step into the pickup.

But she moved up real close to me, and I stepped back. It wasn't like she smelled bad with that perfume she always wears, but it reminded me of how she'd been looking at me in the last couple of years, kind of smiling with that funny look in her eyes and, always, it seemed, touching me.

"If you can wait just a minute, Will, I need to talk to you."

I looked around at the cars churning up the dirt in the parking lot and realized that church had let out, so I knew it was getting kind of late. I would just have time to get home for lunch. And I said so.

"Come sit with me in the car a minute, Will," she said. "Maybe you can allay my fears about something."

I'd have to look up that word 'allay' though I thought I knew what it meant. But I didn't think I ought to sit in her Caddie because of being dirty, afraid I had grease on my Levi's. I told her, too. And that's when she kind of laughed like she was laughing at me. "Are you nervous around girls like this all the time, Will? I think we really need to talk."

So far, I hadn't understood a thing she meant, and she hadn't answered me about the dirty Levi's. So I got in the car and shut the door because I didn't want to get dust in it. It made me nervous just to sit on the furry, leopard-skin seats and to put my boots on the matching light tan floor mats. I noticed even the sun visors were covered in a furry material and, aside from making me feel like I was in a lion's den, I thought the look she was going for cheapened the otherwise classy red and white colors of her new car. And it was new. I could still smell the factory odor, even below what must've been her perfume.

I decided I had to get out, but before I could object, she got in, started the engine, and backed out of the lot. She headed south toward Animas.

"Ma'am. I need to get my pickup and get back home. I don't have time—"

"You'll just have to take a little time, Will," Mrs. Collins said, still laughing kind of mean like, though I guess that's how older people get. They're used to bossing their kids.

So I shut up and just waited. We drove south out of Cotton City, and a mile or so down the road, she turned right onto a farm road and drove down it about a quarter of a mile. She pulled to a stop off to the side and killed the engine.

The alfalfa field we'd parked next to was green and looked nice against the brown of the mountains and the turquoise of the sky. Butterflies flew about in the alfalfa. I fiddled with the window controls to roll my window down, but with the car off, they didn't work, and it was stuffy and close in the Caddie. I felt trapped and was drowning in her perfume. I was nervous, too, because Mrs. Collins looked weird the way she was smiling at me with a gleam in her eyes.

"I've been hearing things, Will," she finally said, looking straight ahead, both hands still on the steering wheel. "Things that make me afraid for you. Things that would just kill your mother if she heard." Then she looked straight at me with that gleam still in her eyes, and she didn't look the least bit afraid. "I just talked to Rick Zumwalt. He and your sister are pretty serious about each other aren't they?"

I noticed how thick her lipstick was and the way it kind of caked at the edges of her mouth, and I wondered if she really thought that looked pretty.

"They'll probably get married, Ma'am." I was confused. I wondered if Mrs. Collins had any idea what it was she wanted to talk about. "But you said you were afraid of something and wanted me to allay your fears? Was it something Rick said? You said you talked to him?"

"This is hard for me," Mrs. Collins said. But it didn't look hard for her at all, because she was still grinning at me, like she was enjoying every minute of it. I was getting so nervous, I was afraid my legs were going to start shaking. I knew there was a spot of grease on my T-shirt, and I was kind of sweaty and stinky, even though the day was cool. I'd been up since dawn and hadn't bathed. And here I was sitting in Mrs. Collins' furry, new Caddie between Animas and Cotton City and needed to be getting home for lunch. Everybody would be waiting on me if I didn't get back soon.

"Look, Ma'am, I don't mean to be rude, or nothing, but if you've got something you need to talk to me about, why don't you come over to our house where we can sit and drink coffee?"

But she shook her head and kind of turned in the seat to face me, then laid her right arm on the back of the seat. I felt her hand hovering at the back of my neck. "You don't understand, Will. This is something your mother should not hear. I've got to tell you, you're in deep trouble, but you act like you don't even know it."

I was getting kind of mad, and I didn't like the way she was acting one bit. "Whatever you think I've done, Ma'am, I'm sure it ain't true. I don't have time to get into trouble like some of the rich folks' kids."

Her eyes flared at that. "Then you just tell me why Rick Zumwalt thinks you're a queer and sleeping with that orphan kid you've got living there. He says you and...Lance, is it?...are sharing a bed under the same roof with your mother, and your father hasn't been dead six months."

My breath just stopped in my chest, and I'm sure the truth of what Mrs. Collins said showed on my face, because all I could do was look her right in the eye thinking maybe I'd heard something wrong. Rick had said that? Had Rita told him? But why would she?

"I can help you, Will," Mrs. Collins was saying. "It's kind of a calling I have."

This time, I knew exactly what she meant, and here I was sitting in her car where nobody was likely to come by for who knew how long.

"I don't need help, Ma'am," I said, knowing where this was headed. "And it ain't none of Rick's business what's going on under my roof. Maybe he's just blowing hot air."

She laughed, sharply, and suddenly grabbed my shoulder. I could see her long, red nails out of the corner of my eye and wondered if she had ever worked a day in her life.

"I can make a man out of you, Will. I know it's hard without your father. A boy your age..." She trailed off and ran her hand down my arm.

I was frozen in the seat, like in a dream when I know I need to run but my legs feel like wood. "Please, Mrs. Collins. This ain't right. I really need to get home."

But she wasn't listening to me, and the look in her eyes had changed to a kind of daze I didn't like. I saw the wrinkles around the edges of her eyes, which the makeup was supposed to hide. In the light of this clear fall day, I could also see red splotches on her face that weren't there a minute ago. "What's right is that you learn to appreciate women, Will."

She was wearing a skirt, one like those I'd seen girls in the high school wear, called a wrap-around or something, and with her left hand, she suddenly pulled the skirt open in a movement that showed me she wasn't wearing a thing underneath, and I got a glimpse of her pubic hair and the slit. And before I could even register what she was doing, she laid her hand on my thigh, squeezed, then grabbed my crotch.

It was just a reflex, but I knocked her hand away. Then I grabbed the door handle and flung the door open hard enough that it rocked on its hinges, and I was out of there. I didn't bother to shut the door or look back as I hit the dirt with my boots and began running back toward the highway.

As I ran, I heard the sound of her car starting up and the angry slide of tires on gravel as she raced the engine and came barreling down the road toward me. I moved off into the weeds against the fence and kept on running. She pulled even with me, slowing down, and laughed at me out the window. "I guess I sure got my answer about you, Will Barnett. A cute kid like you! You need me more than you can guess."

I didn't even glance at her but kept on pumping my legs, feeling angry with her and myself for ever getting in her car.

She continued to drive alongside me, laughing, but it sounded forced. Then she sped up and pulled onto the highway, turning south toward Animas.

My feet and mind were racing as I reached the highway, and without slowing I turned north toward Cotton City and kept on running.

* * *

So, as I write this morning, I know that Lance and I have to brace for things. We're lucky we've had a little time to relax before the crops are ready for harvest and before football season hits. Still, some of my time is taken up with football practice, and Lance does lots of art projects for Mr. Drummond, the art teacher. Maybe we've had enough time to get to know and trust each other before the trouble starts. I can almost feel it coming, though, like thunder rolling off in the distance, getting closer with each lightning strike.

I think our lives will be all right if we just rely on each other. I know he's got emotional problems. Big ones. Like that day that he, Mama, May, and I went to get his stuff over in the company town of Playas and his own mother just let him go without saying anything to him—like "sorry for the hell your home life has been"—or even just good-bye. Looking in from the outside, and always knowing Mama loved us kids, I can't really know Lance's deep hurt.

So as I told Uncle Sean, Lance just needs somebody to love him. And that somebody is me.

Also, I'm sure Lance is homesick for the green and water, the clouds and rain of New Orleans. I remember when I saw him sitting out on that rock ledge, the first thing he told me was how much like hell the country around here looked.

Hurt and homesick or not, I have to give him this: he isn't a slacker when it comes to helping me and May with the farm work. At first, he got sore and got hurt a couple of times, but he never complains, even when we have to get up at four in the morning to get things done before school. He's eager to be a part of my family, to get to know my three sisters, May, Rita, and Trinket, and they feel the same about him. He was a little more standoffish with Mama, at first, but Mama couldn't stop herself from showing him the love he must've missed all his life. So over the past couple of months, as he's settled into our family, he and Mama have developed a kind of mother-son thing. It was self-conscious, maybe, on both their parts—Lance because he was kind of gun-shy about giving out too much affection and risking having it thrown back in his face, and Mama because Lance and I are sleeping together and we haven't denied what that means.

Of course, now I see that's a problem, since everybody in my family knows—even Trinket. She's probably too young to understand, but I bet even if

Mrs. Collins hadn't heard it from Rick Zumwalt, as she said, she would eventually have learned it from Trinket, since my little sister spends the night over there a lot with her friend Julie. May has known from the beginning, and it wasn't long before Rita caught on. That's probably where the real problem came from. Her boyfriend Rick caught on, too, and started out by asking Rita a lot of questions. He's over for supper almost every night of the week, because they're serious about each other. I feel kind of uneasy around him, especially when we're all in the living room visiting. One night, he seemed real interested in Lance, asking where he was from. Lance and I were sitting on the couch together, though not as close as we sit with the family when there's nobody else there. Lance just answered his questions mechanically. He grew tired, even among us, talking about his stepfather and the past, so he gave Rick the facts without offering explanation.

"You have a girlfriend, though?" Rick persisted, looking directly at Lance, then at me, kind of smiling lopsided and curious. I saw Rita's face. She was embarrassed. She caught my eye, and I could see apology there.

So I figured trouble might be coming our way. I just never dreamed Rick would tell Mrs. Collins. I should have figured they would know each other. Although Hachita and Cotton City are in different counties and are forty miles apart, we're so intertwined in this southwest part of the state, everybody knows everybody else. Everybody has gone to the same high school for several years, since they closed the high school in Hachita in 1962. We all know Rick's family, even though he's from over near Cotton City. They're big farmers compared to us. He has a whole bunch of brothers, and his family has been in the area for generations. Rick's been out of school for a year, but he and Rita met in high school. He's a real tough guy and, until yesterday, I thought he was all right—except for his curiosity about me and Lance. After that night when he asked Lance if he had a girlfriend, I got Rita off by herself and asked her point-blank why Rick was so interested. Rita started crying and I felt like wrapping my arms around her. "He figured out about you and Lance, Will. He's not stupid, you know."

"But did you tell him he was right?"

That's when she looked away, and I went real gentle on her saying I understood, though I was angry and my heart was pounding and my breath was short. So I should have known people were going to talk.

I need to backtrack just a little, now that I'm trying to get things down in order.

I'll write it down after supper tonight, when Lance is studying.

* * *

Lance came into our lives two days before Daddy died. That was just this summer in late July. I met him when I was out hiking west of our farm. He had run away from home after his stepfather had beat on him. Then he had wandered in the desert for much of that day and spent the night there. His stepfather was going to work in the Phelps-Dodge copper smelting plant nearby. Lance thought his stepfather had brought him to hell, and with the beating he got the day they arrived, he decided he couldn't take it anymore. But he didn't get far from home and was looking rough by the time I found him. He was ready to fight me off the rock ledge where he was sitting. Only it didn't frighten me a bit, because he was so little. And even though his face was bruised, I could tell he was just about the prettiest boy I'd ever seen. Ever since Uncle Sean had moved off to California, I had been lonely, and from the first time I laid eyes on Lance, I just knew I had to help him.

The last thing Daddy ever talked about with me was letting Lance stay with us, until we could find out more about his situation at home. Daddy didn't like the idea of allowing some other man's runaway child to hide out with us. He didn't want Lance to go back home, either. He died, though, before he had made a decision.

Although Mama might not have wanted Lance to stay with us, he did. He was in a bad way. But without Daddy, it was up to Mama to say whether or not Lance stayed. Only, she was at a loss, probably too stunned by Daddy's death to make a decision. Daddy's death was a shock on all of us. He was sure enough sick, but nobody thought he was going to die on the operating table. He bled to death, like a bicycle tire that has run over too many thorns and is leaking in too many places to repair.

Daddy's death left me with the farm on my shoulders. But with the help of my older sister May, who can drive a tractor as well as I can, and with

Lance there to help me, I figured I could handle the farm and my school work. I had just one more year to go before I graduated. I also had Mama and my two little sisters to worry about. I'm not saying Mama wasn't capable. I'm sure she could have waitressed in Lordsburg or even bar-tended, but I didn't want to see that, so I convinced her that May, Lance, and I could run things. As for my two younger sisters, Rita and Trinket, Rita was fifteen when Lance came to live with us and she was dating the Zumwalt boy and would probably marry right out of high school. Trinket (my youngest sister Shawna) was just coming up on thirteen and needed Mama to be home. So Mama didn't fret over it too much that Lance would be living with us.

So he stayed. Only he was going to be sleeping with me. That's what Mama didn't like, but she just didn't have the strength to resist. Maybe Lance and I were both emotional wrecks, but we fell in love so fast it would make your head spin. It wasn't but a single day after Daddy died when Mama came home that I finally told her about myself. She accused her brother Uncle Sean of making me 'that way,' though it wasn't true.

It's not like me to be disrespectful of Mama. But I just knew Lance needed to be loved. As far as all that goes, like I said, it's turned out all right.

The best thing is Lance sure enough loves me, like I love him. He is the prettiest boy in the school, too. So when school started, everybody wanted to meet him. Girls were saying hi to him, but so were the boys, asking if he was going to play football or track or basketball. Even though he said he liked how friendly everyone was, he was shy and always waited for me by my locker, always had a big smile for me. I saw the girls giggling about him when he passed by, and I teased him about it when we were alone. But he teased back, loosening up more and more, and he would grab my crotch and say, "but girls don't have one of these." Or he would kiss me, gobbling my face and leaving it slick and ask if I could do without that if he started dating.

We loved each other so much, every day was a thrill. Every night was heaven. And at school, he always made a beeline for me between classes and walked close to me and talked excitedly about his classes. So I was happier than I had ever been, and sometimes when we were together in the cafeteria or walking down the hall between classes, I ached to just kiss him right there in front of everybody, like the girl and boy couples did. I wanted to hold his hand, and he told me the same thing.

Like I said, he is beautiful, with his sandy-brown hair, his smooth face, which is almost cleared up from the bruises and welts he had when I first laid eyes on him last summer. He has violet colored eyes of such a silky texture that when he's troubled they turn a violet brown. Like my Uncle Sean, he has soft, pink lips, almost like he's wearing a light shade of lipstick. He's also little for his age. I'm already over six feet and muscled from farming and playing football. But even though he's almost a year older than me, he's a head shorter and has a small body I can completely wrap my arms around in the bed.

So even though we had known each other for just a couple of months, I started talking about being married with him. We were lying in bed one night, just talking after we made love and weren't sleepy, yet. I told him about the two guys Uncle Sean and I had seen in Deming at the movie theater, when we saw "Midnight Cowboy." I told him the two guys wore wedding rings and that I wanted us to get rings, too. At first, Lance just laughed, but after he thought about it, he asked, "you mean like you and me are husband and wife, or something?" kind of giggling and sounding excited about it at the same time.

"No. Like you're my husband, and I'm your husband. No wife."

He laughed at that and rolled over and kissed me then snuggled into my chest, and I wrapped my arms around him, and we fell asleep like that.

Then the next day when we met in the cafeteria at school, we continued to talk about being 'married' over all the noise around us. We were sitting by ourselves side-by-side and were talking about what our last names would be if we really could get married.

He said, "How about 'Surnett,' you know, combining Surfett and Barnett?"

"Or 'Barfett,'" I said.

Then we both doubled over, howling with laughter.

It wasn't until I straightened up and wiped the tears from my eyes that I saw heads were turned near us, and I met Dick Lamb's eyes a few tables away. I was still grinning from ear-to-ear and, when our eyes locked, it was like he was waiting for that as an excuse to come over and talk to me. He was sitting with the rest of the football team, and they were all staring at us. That's when I noticed that Casey Zumwalt, Rick's youngest brother, was sitting with the other team members, and I remembered how interested Rick had been in Lance a few nights before. So when Dick got up and nodded at them and they nodded back, I thought, "Uh, oh," and recalled how Rick had kind of grinned at me after supper and asked Lance if he had a girlfriend.

So Dick came over and sat down in an empty chair on the other side of Lance. Lance and I were sitting close with our shoulders touching, but when Dick sat down, Lance leaned back and I leaned forward. "What's up, buddy?" I said to Dick. I couldn't keep the grin off my face, still thinking how funny 'Barfett' was, but Dick was frowning.

"Me and the guys've been talking about you," he said, some of his frown turning into curiosity, and I remembered the day in the showers a couple of years before when he'd asked if I was queer for my Uncle Sean because of how I always wore his dog tags.

"Good things, I hope." But I knew it wasn't.

Dick glanced back toward the other guys. Then he leaned in real close like he was going to whisper something, so I had to put my arm around Lance to lean a little closer to Dick.

"Hey, you know I like you," Dick said. "And I like Lance, too, seeing as how he's kind of like an orphan and your mother's taken him in."

I gave Lance's shoulder a squeeze and our legs touched under the table. "Yeah? We like you, too, buddy."

At that he smiled a little. "Well, the guys have been talking, you know? Wondering just what it is between you and Lance. I've tried to tell 'em you're cool, but some of 'em think it's a little queer the way you and Lance—"

"Not that again, Dick! Geez! Don't you ever give up?" I couldn't think of anything else to say. At the table of football players, I saw that Casey had a lopsided grin on his face, just like his older brother had grinned the other night. I wasn't going to go apeshit on Dick, though, because I figured he was just like me and Lance, only having some hell of a hard time admitting it, and maybe the other guys had put Dick up to it because of how he had been the first to make an issue out of me possibly being queer. And here it was again.

"Well, Will, you have to admit you and Lance act like nobody else exists. Don't freeze us out. We're all on the same team."

"One thing," I said, raising my voice just a little. "Quit talking about Lance as if he's not here."

"It's okay," Lance said. I felt his leg shaking a little. He didn't like the kind of talk Dick was telling us about and neither did I, but I didn't know what to do about it.

"Sorry," Dick said, turning to Lance. "You're just as involved in this as Will is." Then back to me: "It's just you keep giving the wrong impression, Will. Everybody knows you ain't never had no girlfriend."

"Who are you, Dear Abby? It's nobody's business if you ask me," I said. I wasn't about to pretend I even wanted a girlfriend, and I wasn't going to make any lame excuses, either.

Dick looked troubled. "Can't say I didn't warn you, either of you guys." Then he just got up and headed out of the cafeteria. A moment later, the bell rang and made me jump. I still had my arm around Lance's shoulder, and I was close enough I could have pecked him on the cheek. I almost did.

"You okay?" I asked. "Does it bother you what Dick says?"

Lance shook his head and turned to me. Our mouths were only about six inches apart, and I could feel his breath on my face. "I love you, Will," he whispered. "Long as we don't hold hands or kiss around school, it's just talk, right?"

"Damn right!" I said, though I knew it was a lot more than just talk. "See you after school? You gonna come watch me practice?"

Lance shook his head and began to gather up his books. We both got up. "I've gotta study for my math test, and I've got some artwork to do for Mr. Drummond. Posters for the first home game. Meet ya' at the pickup."

So, as the days passed, I could feel things beginning to tighten down a little. Still, every day was so fresh and new getting to know Lance, to see that even with some of the guys yacking about us, he wasn't a pussy about it, which made me proud. I still had that ideal from the two guys I had seen in Deming wearing wedding bands, standing in line at the movies with their arms around each other's shoulders. Besides, there wasn't anything specifically 'queer' about two guys arm-in-arm.

Talking to Uncle Sean about things like this gave me a little more courage, though it didn't reduce my fear.

"You're tough, Will, and your friends won't believe it."

"But there's talk," I said.

"That's all it is. Just remember that most of them think queers are effeminate—and you're surely not a sissy, okay?"

What he said made some sense because, when guys tease each other about being queer, they usually make their voices go high like a girl's and prance around like a sissy.

Still, it wasn't easy to relax. It might be "just talk," as Uncle Sean said, but it was also true.

Every day that I had football practice, and if Lance wasn't doing anything for art class, he came out to the football field and sat up in the bleachers that lined the east side of our small stadium and watched us. The coach didn't mind other kids watching, though it was usually girls watching their boyfriends. Most of the guys were on the football team or had basketball practice. So it might have been a little odd for Lance to be just about the only guy there. But it made me feel good, and just like the other guys whose girlfriends were out there, I could show off in front of Lance.

Like I said before, every man's son for miles around tried to get into athletics at Animas High. But football is the supreme game, and Coach is generous in letting every guy who wants try out for the team. If they can stick with it, he lets them be part of the team in some way. I hadn't played my freshman year, since I had been so screwed up over Uncle Sean leaving; but this was my third year in football and, just as Dick Lamb had said, I was part of the team. So after the talk started, the only thing I could think of was to not freeze anyone else out because of Lance.

So, one day, I brought him into the locker room when we were all suiting up for practice. It wasn't as easy to divert the suspicions as it had been that first year in football because, back then, I didn't have a boyfriend and people like Rick Zumwalt had no idea about me. Most of the guys shook hands with Lance, though a few of them smirked. When Lance stuck out his hand to shake Casey's, Casey was a real asshole, gripping Lance's hand so hard I could see the pain on his face. Then, when Casey finally released his grip, he grinned: "Maybe Will ain't workin' you hard enough on the farm, there, Lance. You got a grip like a girl."

So, later, on the field, I deliberately knocked Casey around. Even though I'm a wide receiver and shouldn't even be making body contact with the line, I found a way to punish him. He got a little punch-drunk, too, which would've made me laugh, but I knew he'd meant to embarrass Lance. Coach Grey kept getting on my case that I wasn't playing my position, but I ignored him. When we were almost finished with practice, I rammed into Casey one last time, knocking him flat on his back, and leaned over him, sweat dripping off my face onto his. When I knew I had his attention, I said, "I guess you must be the runt of your family, there, Casey. It's as easy to knock you over as it is a sick calf. You get my message?"

"Fuck you, faggot!" Casey wheezed like an old man.

"Just keep your dirty thoughts to yourself. You don't, and I'll work you over like this every day."

I didn't feel a bit better, though. It's like my daddy always said: Wanting to get revenge and getting it are two different things; once you have your revenge, you feel ashamed. And I did.

* * *

So, here it is. Maybe I was stupid, now that I think about it. Maybe if I hadn't got on Casey that day, Rick might not have told Mrs. Collins that Lance and I were sleeping together. I guess that's what made Mrs. Collins think she could get in my pants to make a man out of me. I know she didn't really care about me. She just wanted to get my young dick as a kind of trophy. I'm sure refusing her advances made things worse. Who knows, now, who she's been telling about the incident?

# Three
# At the Pep Rally

I studied Mama at breakfast, wondering if Margie Collins had said anything to her, yet. But I didn't think so because she didn't look bothered about anything. She just looked tired, sitting there in her blue terry-cloth robe at the table with a cup of coffee and smoking a cigarette. She'd beat everyone but me out of bed and had breakfast set out on the counter by the sink. Since things had settled down with Lance living with us, and he and Mama sure enough liked each other, she smiled at him when he came in, just as she did the rest of us. I watched him, too, and decided I had to tell him what happened between me and Margie Collins. Although it was still calm at school, Casey kept smirking at me and had a gleam in his eye, so I figured Casey knew from his brother how Mrs. Collins had tested me and how I had flunked.

I also figured Mrs. Collins was mad about what happened, because her daughter Julie called and said her mother wasn't going to be coming by today to take Trinket to the bus stop. So as tired as Mama was, she left the kitchen to get dressed so she could take Trinket the near ten miles where the bus for the elementary/middle school passes each morning heading into Hachita.

Rita would be getting a ride with Rick, and I wanted to be long gone before he showed up. But I threw everybody off when I told May I wanted her to come with Lance and me. I had decided May needed to know about things.

"But Kelsey can give me a ride, Will," she said. "You're gonna put yourself late. I'm not even showered yet."

"Call her, May," I said, "and tell her I'm giving you a ride." Our eyes met and she nodded, realizing I wasn't just offering for the heck of it. May had been lucky, now that she had graduated school, to get a job as the assistant girl's coach. Of course, it wasn't exactly standard, but in a small school like Animas they sometimes have to waive the rules and hire people from the community to fill some of their needs. Her friend Kelsey Snow, who I had finally figured out was like me and May, usually gave May a ride all the way to Animas, even though Kelsey worked in Hachita at the Hachita Grill. Same thing after work. They usually didn't get home until well after dark, so I figured they were dating, but May wouldn't talk to me about it.

Even though Lance and I would be a little late, it didn't matter today. The high school was having a pep rally to kick off the first football game of the season—a home game. We were playing Lordsburg on our field.

So when we were in the pickup with Lance in the middle and May on the outside, heading into Hachita, I told them what Mrs. Collins had done to me.

Lance was quiet, I guess, trying to take in what I had said, but May screamed in anger and laughed at the same time. "That slut!" she said. "You mean she pulled off her skirt and showed you her bush?"

I wasn't laughing, and I felt Lance tense up at the news. I could tell he was tense because, even though we didn't hide our affection in front of May, he held onto my thigh like he was about to fall. I glanced from him to May.

"If bush is what you call it. Yeah, she showed it to me," I said. "I was so shocked, it wasn't until she rubbed my crotch that I bolted."

May's face, which is splattered with freckles, went red with anger, or maybe embarrassment. No, not embarrassment. Not May. "You should have slapped her face, Will, you know that? An old woman like her? But I knew she had the hots for you just like she did Uncle Sean."

"That's what I thought, too," I told her. "I can't believe she'd go as far as she did. I'm afraid it'll ruin things between her and Mama. So I don't think I should tell Mama."

"It's more than talk, now." Lance spoke so quietly, I glanced from the road and into his face and caught his eyes. They were troubled and going from that lovely violet to a darker shade. "Everybody's gonna know, Will," he said, digging his fingers into my leg.

May and I exchanged glances, and I saw that she was just as worried as I was. We were both protective of Lance, and he seemed so quietly frightened, I didn't know how he was going to take it if a storm did blow through the school. He'd already been embarrassed in front of the team the way Casey did him that day. And if Rick had told Mrs. Collins about me and Lance because Casey had whined about the way I'd knocked him around on the football field, I could just imagine what they'd do if I tried to get back at them, now.

* * *

Animas High School faces east. It sits on a street west of the main highway that runs south through Animas from Cotton City and continues on down to the boot heel of New Mexico. When we arrived at the school we headed straight for the football stadium on the west side of the high school. The pep rally was about to start and the parking lot between the stadium and the high school building was crammed with pickup trucks and cars. I recognized many of them as we wove our way through the lot for the stadium. Some belonged to people who had already graduated and had stayed in the area, like Rick Zumwalt. And I guess I would probably go to the pep rallies and the games, too, if I were going to stay here after I graduated from high school.

In the stadium, the band was just messing around as they tuned up. The drummers were going full tilt with the rhythm they set up when we were gaining yardage one scrimmage at a time. We came in through the south entrance and had to stand off to the side because the seats were already full. We have the smallest seating of any of the high schools. Going to Deming is like going off to a bowl game in comparison. But we only play them every couple of years, depending on their schedule and not ours. I don't think they like being whipped by a smaller school. Across the field my teammates were also standing. They had suited up, but because I was late, I decided I wouldn't. I was looking around and, before I could pretend I hadn't seen her, my eyes met Margie Collins', staring straight at me and smirking. She grinned and ran her tongue over her smeary red lips.

As usual, the whole school had turned out. Many of the students were there because it was like a recess, but most of them were real fans of the games. When the cheerleaders led the first cheer, the crowd exploded and the band jumped into "Hold that Tiger," though we sang "hold that panther!"

Lance had told me he'd gone to a huge high school in New Orleans and had never once been to a pep rally or one of his school's games. Now, he just looked around, almost indifferently, and I doubted that he would ever really catch the fever that sports caused in the people of this small town.

Then the principal began announcing the names of the players in the upcoming home game, and one-by-one my teammates stepped forward and raised both hands while the crowd clapped, or guys called out stuff that made the crowd laugh. When my name was called, the crowd was looking toward the other players, but I stepped out, anyway, from the other side of the field holding my hands up.

"BARNETT'S GOT A BOYFRIEND!" some guy called out, and every word came out so clear, I knew the whole crowd heard. A second later, someone started booing, then a few more people joined in. It was strange, however, that most of the crowd was just quiet. Then the principal called out the next guy's name, which just happened to be Dick Lamb, and when he stepped out from among his teammates, a roar went up across the stadium because he was our star player, our quarterback. The year before, he had thrown passes like rockets that hit their targets almost every time.

I was glad I'd been passed over quickly because, when I heard what the guy had yelled and then the booing, I didn't know if it was to boo him or to boo me. When I moved back next to Lance, he looked frightened and had gone a little pale. When I touched his shoulder, he jerked it away and turned and ran out of the stadium.

The last thing I heard before I ran out after him—noticing that people were looking at us—was the beginning of another cheer.

It felt odd to be upset under a clear blue sky with a light breeze coming from the north, hinting at fall. I heard the trumpets and drum beats of the marching band back in the stadium. This was my last season as a football player. Not that I was really all that good, though I was able to connect with Dick's passes and gain a few yards each game. But something had changed this morning, something I didn't think I could tease my way through. Someone had called out my secret with Lance, which I guess I never really bothered to keep secret, since my family knew—and Rick and Mrs. Collins, and Rick's brother Casey. Now, at the pep rally, someone had put a name to our secret, and here I was running with my chest full of fear—not down the field, attempting to make a touchdown before I'm hauled to the ground by my opponents—but running into the high school building, afraid that Lance and I would be hauled down by rumor and cruelty. I caught a glimpse of him as he disappeared down the main hallway. I blasted through the double doors and skidded to a stop, glancing around. I saw Lance enter Mr. Drummond's classroom. So I tried to catch my breath, tried to calm myself down. The pep rally would be going on until ten, and it was just now eight-thirty.

I couldn't go into Mr. Drummond's class, afraid that he was there. Art class was Lance's sanctuary when he and I couldn't be together, and I wasn't going to ruin it for him by bursting in and startling Mr. Drummond. I looked in through the pane of glass in the door. Lance was flipping through some of his drawings in the sketchbook I'd bought him. Then I saw the Barker twins, both girls, who had come in from Playas, whose own fathers had been hired at the smelter plant where Lance's stepfather worked. They were artistic, as well, and were just about the only girls Lance had made real friends with.

I was about to walk away when Lance looked toward the door, saw me looking through the glass, and grabbed up his stuff, sketchpad included, and came out into the hall.

He still looked frightened and confused but he attempted a smile, which I appreciated. "Sorry I ran out on you, Angel," he said in his oily southern drawl, "but when that guy screamed out about us, I remembered these…" He pulled the sketchpad from under his arm and flipped a few pages, past blanks, then stopped and opened the book for me to see.

"I thought I better pull these out and give them to you." Our eyes met, and then I looked at the drawings.

There I was in all my (imagined) glory, naked as a mesquite in winter. Lance had done me more than justice and bulked me up a little. He had brought my left thigh up on the stool I was (supposedly) sitting on to discreetly hide our "little buddy." Then he flipped the page and there I was again, this time reclining on the bank of the cow pond on Old Man Hill's place. In the picture, the pond is encircled by weeping willows. Shadow and light illuminate my body, and this time our little buddy is asleep, but visible beneath the shadow of a weeping willow branch that shades my crotch. When he flipped to a third picture, I couldn't keep from laughing, and he frowned up at me as he removed the drawings from the tablet and rolled them into a tube.

"You need to put these in the pickup, Will. I don't want someone to find them when they're snooping around."

"People do that in here?"

Lance grinned. "We've all done nude studies. So we like to peek at each other's stuff. Only I thought since people are talking, it wouldn't be a good idea if someone saw them."

I felt sorry for Lance and was secretly flattered that he would use me as a nude study at school. I felt sorry for him because I didn't think he was ready to face the mean things some of the students might say to him, now, if people were going to broadcast the news about us. After the pep rally, a few students came up to me in the hall between classes and said they'd heard the remark about me having a boyfriend, though I couldn't tell if they told me to embarrass me or just to let me know. Funny that no one knew exactly who had said it, but as I say, we even get people from the community who have already graduated coming to the pep rallies, and it could have been someone from Cotton City who knows Rick. In a way that's better than having someone from the school spreading the rumors about me and Lance; but in another way, it's bad, because it means that Rick (probably) is telling other people besides Margie Collins.

As I write this, it's after supper. Lance and Trinket are putting together a jigsaw puzzle in the living room. May isn't back yet. I bet she's out with Kelsey. And of course Rita's not here. I wonder if she and Rick still talk about me and Lance. Rita said she felt guilty because of how Rick found out. I haven't told her about Mrs. Collins, yet—although Rick might have already told her. I'll just have to wait and see. I guess the only person I really don't want to know is Mama. She's been great with me and Lance, even though I'm sure it hurts her, so she'd probably feel obligated to break off her friendship with Mrs. Collins. If things blow over on that side, I'll be relieved because I would hate to see Mama and Mrs. Collins break up as friends over what happened.

Out here on the farm, twenty miles from Hachita, and even farther from Animas and Cotton City, it's hard to recall how tense I felt all day at school. Although the nights are crisper, I have the window open, and I can feel the softness of the night, hear the desert outside and the noises from inside the rest of the house and feel relaxed.

The first game is two days away. I hope the rumors have died down by then.

# *Four*
# *The Storm and Its Aftermath*

I can't sleep after a game. But tonight it's more than just the game. As usual, my body's worn out, but deep down past the muscle aches, after a good shower, I feel physically good. I'm just too shook up to sleep. Lance is asleep in our bedroom because he's too shook up not to sleep. I'm sitting at the kitchen table. Mama, May, Trinket, and Rita are in bed, too. May has taken over Uncle Sean's room (where my oldest sisters Julianne and Marsha slept when they were living at home). Rita resents having to share a room with Trinket, claiming she's too old to be nagged by her baby sister.

Only Trinket doesn't nag anymore. She's had to grow up fast, first with Daddy dying, and now with Lance living here and people knowing about us. She has seen how mean some people can be. She met Lance when he had been freshly beat up by his stepfather, and now she's got to make sense out of what happened to him after the football game tonight. She'll see his lip is busted, and we'll have to come up with something that will make sense to her, without letting her know how close Lance came to getting hurt really bad. We'll have to come up with something to tell Mama, too, so she won't fret. I've got to make sense of what happened as well, though I've got to wait until Monday to find out more from other people. Find out what they saw.

A home game is the biggest event in Hachita, Animas, and Cotton City, and tonight was no different. Our stadium only has one set of bleachers on the east side of the field. But people come from all over and most of them watch the game standing up. The bands for each school play on opposite sides of the field.

This was the first time Lance saw me play against another team. Trinket once told him that I was Dick Lamb's star receiver, and she believed it more than I did. I am pretty good at snagging his passes, though, even if I'm about to fall from a double take-down. So it felt good to know that Lance was up in the stands. He and Mama and Trinket got to sit in the bleachers as family members of the players. Those who made the decision at the ticket booth already knew about Lance being kind of an orphan. Some people might have even known about his stepfather beating on him. Lance had never made that a secret when other students struck up conversations with him as the new kid in school. Fact is, there were several new students this year who started with Lance because of the new town of Playas that went in. Although most of them went to the lower grades, the hallway still feels more full during the day. And the stadium seemed packed and noisy tonight as our team took the field for introductions. I figured people from Playas were at the game, too.

Each guy ran out waving his arms as his name was called, trotting over to the middle of the field and taking his place by his teammates. When my name was called, I hesitated a split second, feeling my face turn red, expecting catcalls as there had been at the pep rally a few days before.

When my name echoed from the loud speakers above the bleachers, I ran out onto the field. Normally, my heart swelled to hear my name, then the cheering of the crowd. But tonight, I listened for derision and booing and ran quickly to my place in the line, relieved that there was only cheering. We stood facing the bleachers, and I scanned the crowd for Lance, easily finding his face in the glare of the lights. When our eyes met, Lance and I raised our hands at the same moment and waved to each other.

"—blowing kisses to his boyfriend," Casey said, under his breath to Dick, who snorted at Casey's wit.

I heard it but pretended I didn't.

A few minutes later, the game began with the bugle call to "charge" as we became the receivers, and I caught the kick and bulldozed my way across the field making it almost to the fifty yard line. The cheering crowd, the band, the announcer's voice blurred into the first prickles of sweat as we danced and grunted our way down field. We made the first touchdown in two plays.

Back from the line, I could hear the linemen threaten and taunt each other as they waited for the snap, but I was listening more closely to Dick's countdown of the play. As a back fielder, however, I am removed from the hand-to-hand combat at the line, so I scanned the lineup and went into motion when the snap came, cutting past the line and running out unopposed for a few seconds, hoping Dick would recover and pass quickly.

Only tonight, he kept passing to Ronald Spencer, the other receiver, whether he was open or not, and during half-time I laid into Dick.

"What the hell do you think you're doing, Dick! I've been open all night and you won't even look in my direction!"

We were shirtless and drenching ourselves with water, then toweling off, waiting for Coach to come in.

He shoved me. "Mind your own business, Barnett. I'm doing my job as I see it."

"And you don't see me, ready to waltz into the end-zone? You're blind or stupid!"

"He don't want to get faggot sweat on the ball," Casey Zumwalt said. He'd been watching Dick and me argue.

"Is that it, huh? Is it, Dick?" I said, glancing at Casey, then glaring at Dick. "You're all nervous over what Casey says. How do you even know it's true?"

Dick and Casey exchanged glances. Dick smirked. "Yeah, Barnett, it is that," he said.

I caught his eyes, made him look at me. "Really?"

"Anybody that turns down free pussy has to be queer," he said.

So I knew right then that Mrs. Collins had been talking. As we returned to the field, I had a lump in my stomach that wouldn't go away. The drums sounded like thunder. The storm was getting closer.

* * *

"Pass it to Barnett! You idiot! Barnett's wide open!"

It was the second half, coming up on the end of the third quarter. I was glad someone saw what was going on. I wouldn't have minded that Dick wasn't hitting me, except Spencer was messing up, and Dick's throwing arm was soft tonight.

We lost on our home field, not that Lamb passing it to me would necessarily have changed the outcome, but we missed several opportunities, and it made me mad to think Dick would risk throwing a game down the toilet just to show me what he thought of me.

Coach Grey laid into him during one of our time-outs, but even he had a funny look on his face and didn't look at me, at all.

The game ended and we left the field hanging our heads.

"What they get for having a faggot on the field!" someone said from the other team.

"Damn right, man," his teammate said. "Makes me sick to my stomach!"

I knew who the guys were. We always played Lordsburg for the first home game, so it was embarrassing to have lost tonight, especially on our own turf, because Lordsburg is not as good as we are in football. They sounded pumped up and proud and mean-spirited, so I just slunk back to the locker room to shower.

I noticed that Dick and Casey were already showered and gone by the time I got there, so I hoped Lance would meet me in the locker room after my shower. The other guys on the team were still friendly to me, showing by their slaps on the back and their lowered eyes they thought Lamb had messed up too. So if Lance came in as usual, we could put on a brave face. Despite the rumors, at least these guys would see that the talk didn't bother us.

But Lance didn't come.

So I figured he was waiting for me in the stadium parking lot.

The cars were still milling around and raising dust, and even though it was nippy out, I was only wearing a T-shirt. I'd left my Levi jacket in the pickup, so even though I didn't see Lance, I headed for the pickup to retrieve it. When I opened the door I had to step back, almost gagging. Someone had thrown fresh cow manure onto the seat. That wouldn't be hard to come by, since almost every kid who goes to school, here, comes from a farm or ranch.

* * *

I didn't know what to do. It would be hard to clean up the cow manure in the dark. Daddy had covered the seats with plastic a few years before, so we could clean off the grease and stuff, and since I used the pickup to go back and forth to school and run errands, I kept it clean. I was too worried about where Lance might be, however, to try cleaning off the cow manure, so I locked the pickup so he couldn't get in and accidentally sit on it and headed for the school building.

There was a dance going on in the gymnasium after the game. I never went. I didn't know how to dance, and I never dated, anyway, so it didn't matter. I was also sure that was the last place I'd find Lance, so I headed for Mr. Drummond's classroom. Lance might be there if he was upset, though I didn't know why he might be, since nothing really happened at the game, other than us losing.

He wasn't there.

The lump of dread in my stomach grew a little heavier. I tried to remember if Lance had told me where he'd meet me. Only there just wasn't anywhere else he would normally be, so I went back out to the parking lot to try to figure out some way to clean up the cow manure. I was tired and wanted to start home because, after dark, the fifty miles seems long.

Back at the pickup, I unlocked the passenger-side door and opened the glove box where I keep a flashlight. There was cow manure in the seat all right, a big, green, ten-pound, stinking pile of it; but I had lucked out. Most of it had landed on my Levi jacket, which was laying on the seat. So I slid the jacket out on the passenger side, then stepping backward, and quickly pivoting, I slung the jacket out over the other cars still there. I heard it come to a sloppy, wet stop on what sounded like the hood of a car.

People would recognize the jacket.

I just didn't care.

The lump grew heavier, and I was getting worried. Lance could have gone home with Mama and Trinket, since Mama drove tonight. So I went back in the hallway at the school and dropped a dime in the box at the payphone by the principal's office. Off toward the gymnasium, I could hear the pounding of the music and the noise of the crowd.

The phone rang about ten times before I hung up, realizing Mama wouldn't have had time to get home, yet.

That's when Casey Zumwalt came into the brightly lit hallway. He looked like he was about to puke, and when he saw me, the darkest look of fear animated his face.

"God! Will! I'm glad I found you!" Casey said, sounding pumped with hysteria.

It scared me and I began to shake. "It's Lance, isn't it?"

He just nodded, and put up both hands toward me, as if he were warding me off. "Locker room," he said, turning and running back down the hall. "The girls' locker room!" he shouted, as he shoved open the double doors at the end and stepped out into the night.

I crashed through the same doors. Within a few seconds, I was across the parking lot and skidding around the bleachers. When I got to the girls' locker room, I threw open the outer door and ran inside. Here, the lights were off except for the dim night lights in metal cages inside the showers. The place was empty.

I wondered if Casey was just putting on an act since he never liked Lance. But I shook off that thought, because he had been genuinely scared. I was more worried than ever, and started to run back out, having no idea what I should do. That's when I heard Lance's unmistakable whimpering coming from the showers—a sound I sometimes hear at night when he's sleeping and dreaming about what must be one of his stepfather's beatings, or some other kind of deep pain. The whimpering sound just tears me up. There's no spelling for it, no vowels to encompass it.

As I rounded the corner, I felt for the light switch, then flicked it on. At first I couldn't tell what I was looking at, then I realized that Lance was lying in a heap of torn and disheveled clothing, his pants and underwear shoved down around his calves, his shirt ripped open from the back, his bare bottom red and splotched, and I was afraid to see his face.

I sat down by him and rolled him into my lap. His head lolled forward, then kind of jerked, and he moaned. He was unconscious. His bottom lip was swollen and had been split on the lower right side. I hugged him to my chest, feeling the tears well up in my eyes. "Not again!" I whispered. "Why do they always go for your beautiful face!"

I rocked him back and forth, finally relieved to see him awaken. But when he was conscious, he began to flail his arms and shout: "No! No. No!"

So I held tighter. "It's me, Lance! It's Will!"

When he heard my voice, something inside seemed to snap him into full consciousness. He scrambled out of my arms and began pulling up his pants. That's when I saw a trickle of blood on his thigh.

"Wait!" I said, as I scrambled to my feet. I grabbed his hands and he tried to fight me.

"Let me dress, Will! This is embarrassing. Why—
"

"You're bleeding," I said. "Let me see what it is."

So, instead of pulling his clothing on, he sat down and I helped him out of his sneakers and pulled his pants and underwear off. He laid back, beginning to shiver. My own hands were shaking as I gently pushed his thighs apart. In the glare of the lights, his legs were ghostly white, and the thin line of blood was dark on his inner thigh.

I wiped the blood away with my fingers but couldn't see where the bleeding came from.

"Where does it hurt, Lance? I can't—"

Lance pulled up his balls. "It kind of stings, here," he said. He was looking down at himself but couldn't see.

I did.

I tried to keep my face from revealing the horror of what I saw and fought to keep from puking. He wasn't cut badly, and the bleeding had already stopped, but it wasn't that which sickened and frightened me. It was what appeared to have almost been done.

A thin cut—unmistakably from a knife blade—had been made at the base of his ball sac, just enough to cause a little bleeding.

"It burns down there," Lance said, again. "What is it?"

I didn't want to tell him what I suspected. "Someone must've scratched you down here," I said, trying to keep my voice steady, because I knew it wasn't just a scratch.

I wiped away the blood and held his balls, gently pushing the side of my forefinger against the cut, then brought my finger up to the light. I was relieved to see that he wasn't still bleeding.

Then I helped him get dressed.

Anger and hatred burned in his eyes as he looked at me. For a moment, I was afraid he was angry with me.

Then, as I stood up, he came into my arms and began to cry.

"They tried to rape me!" he said, into my shoulder, and I could feel his hot breath on my neck. I held him tight.

"Who, Lance?"

He pulled himself out of my arms, looking up at me, his face so pitiful with bruised lips and the fear still shining in his eyes. "I don't know! They jumped me from behind, but I didn't recognize their voices."

"Not Dick Lamb, or Casey? None of the guys on the team?"

Lance shook his head, then dropped his eyes. "They called me your wife! They said they'd show me what real guys do with girls."

My mind was racing. If Lance didn't know who it was, then they didn't go to school at Animas—though they could've been guys from Lordsburg, or even townspeople. Of course, I probably would've known who the attackers were, since I'd lived here all my life. So my bets lay on a Cotton City bunch. I would've bet on Rick, except Lance knew his voice. The chances were slimmer that it was other high school boys from Lordsburg. Still, I'd know a lot of them, too, since we played them in football and basketball.

"Are you hurt anywhere besides your lips and that scratch?"

Lance nodded, looking distracted. "My ass burns. I think they were slapping me or something, only I blacked out. I'd do that when my stepfather started in. Sometimes the first slug and I was out cold."

He said it so matter-of-factly, yet it wrenched my heart. I knew it wasn't the physical pain that made him faint, however. I'd seen him bloody his knuckles when a wrench slipped and he caught his hand between it and a plow blade. He'd curse and throw the wrench, and suck on his knuckles, but he wouldn't faint. I think when violence is directed at him, he's stunned into unconsciousness, like a hammer blow to his brain. Kind of self-preservation.

So at night, when he's sleeping, and he gives voice to the pain and hurt of his life, I hold him until his breathing is regular, his voice quiet.

"We need to get home," I said. "We need to find out who did this. I think I already know who might have started it."

***

The dance was still going on when we left. It was around eleven-thirty. Tomorrow would be Saturday, for which I was relieved. We were waiting on Trujillo to come by with his combine to harvest the grain, but I doubted it would be this weekend, and I was relieved about that, too. Lance needed a chance to relax after tonight. I doubted, however, that he would ever feel quite as safe at school as he might have away from his stepfather—already beat on by thugs just a few months after running away from home. I swore to myself this would be the last time in his life.

As we drove the fifty miles home from Animas to the farm, Lance lay against my chest under my arm. Occasionally, as we climbed a hill or turned a curve in the road, I had to take my arm from around him and shift up or down. But we were used to this accommodation by now, and it was almost unconscious on our parts.

The hum of the motor and the whine of the tires on the pavement, the gentle swaying of the pickup as we traveled over the highway, the warmth of Lance against me—all these sensations were familiar, comforting, but my mind snagged on how quickly that could change.

When I'd found Lance with his clothing ripped and his pants shoved down around his calves, I was afraid he'd been raped, but he'd said his attackers had tried to rape him. There was a difference—a big one—and I wanted to hope that, out of a night of such violation against him, he had been lucky and escaped such humiliation. "And you're sure they didn't...you know...do things to you?"

He laughed at that. "Angel, I think I would know if someone had done that!"

In the dark, it was hard to tell if his face matched the laugh in his voice. I didn't think so and pulled him tightly against me.

A moment later, he was crying quietly.

"Can you talk about it?"

He sniffled and put an arm around my chest. "I was on my way to the locker room after the game ended. I told your mom and Trinket I'd be riding home with you, so I came down off the bleachers on the north side. People in the crowd were so angry, I heard them cursing the quarterback for not throwing you passes. But I also heard people talking about you and me. Anyway, I got to the bottom and the crowd forced me toward the north entrance, where the girls' locker room and showers are."

Lance sat up out of my arms and I glanced at him. His hair was disheveled. He was staring out the front of the cab at the black and silver of the desert night.

"Someone mentioned me, the 'orphan kid,' and I just kept walking, not thinking too much about that, but as I got close to the locker room, someone grabbed me from behind, and before I knew it, they'd shoved me through the door."

When he turned to look at me and his eyes caught the dash lights, I saw they were pooled with tears. "I thought I saw Casey and Dick behind me, just before that, but it wasn't their voices in the locker room. I tried several times to break free, but someone was squeezing my elbows together behind my back. When I tried to scream for help, someone covered my mouth with his hand, and when I bit down on his fingers, that's when I got hit in the mouth."

"And you didn't faint right then?"

Lance leaned back into the seat. "I'm a lot stronger than I was when we first met," he said, his voice sounding defiant. "I tried to fight back, Will. I knew they weren't going to just let me go."

We were nearing the turn off to the town of Playas. Every time I passed this way, my blood boiled at Lance's parents, but especially his stepfather. The road cut off to the right, toward the south, a darkly glimmering strip of asphalt in the night, and up on the side of the hill where the new town of Playas lay, just a few lights were still lit this late. A moment later, we passed a hill and the town disappeared. From there it was a straight stretch of highway, east into Hachita.

"You didn't see either Dick or Casey after that?"

Again, Lance just shook his head. "Once we were in the locker room, all I could hear were the guys who'd forced me to go with them. 'Let's cornhole this fucker!' one of them said, and they all laughed. 'No, let's make a woman out of him for Barnett.'"

At that, my heart almost stopped, recalling the cut on his ball sac. Calves that have been castrated aren't considered male, and the ranch and farm way of life around here influences the way guys think of themselves—as bulls and stallions. They decided they needed to do something to him. One of us had to be a 'woman' to make things right in their twisted minds.

It struck me that Casey must have been in the locker room and saw something that scared him into going for help. If he had seen the flash of a knife blade and guessed what one of them planned to do, that would account for why he looked so frightened. Was Lance passed out by then? Had they already started ripping his clothes off? Had Casey seen one of them take out a knife? When I got there, Lance was by himself, so something must have happened to scare his attackers off. I couldn't imagine what, and so I knew I had to make Casey tell me what he knew.

"What's the last thing you remember, then?" I asked Lance. I pulled him back down to my chest. I couldn't stand how small and vulnerable he looked over in the seat by himself.

"One of them hitting me with something on the ass. It hurt, Will, and that's when I went nuts, trying to get loose, and someone grabbed my balls and squeezed so hard it was like being kicked in slow motion, and that's the last thing I remember."

"Did you see any of their faces? Or get an idea how many there were?"

He shook his head against my chest.

* * *

When we got home, I was bone tired and angry, and Lance was jumpy and jittery, and when we sat down at the kitchen table for peanut butter and jelly sandwiches, he wouldn't look me in the eye. It must've been after midnight and Mama and Trinket were probably asleep, so I tried to be quiet as I opened the refrigerator for the milk carton. Lance dabbed the peanut butter on a piece of bread, followed by a generous dollop of strawberry jam, as red as his bruised lips. I set the milk on the table, then leaned down behind him and wrapped my arms around him, kissing the top of his head.

"What else is bothering you?"

"Nothing. I'm just scared and mad." He bit into the sandwich, and jam oozed down the right side of his mouth, shiny under the kitchen light. I leaned over and licked it off his chin. Then I kneeled to his side and made him look me in the eyes.

The violet was gone, partly because of the glare of light above us, partly because of his emotional state. "You look sad, too."

He took another bite of his sandwich, wolfing it down, and drank milk out of the carton. He handed it to me and I did the same. He watched me, still looking sad. "If I had been raped, Will…would you still…love me?"

"Of course I would! How can you even ask such a thing?"

"I needed to know. I know you didn't like hearing about the other men I've been with."

I kissed him on the lips, trying to be careful of where it was split, and I tasted the sweet of the jam and the warmth of the peanut butter, the salt of the blood. "They don't matter. You do. I'm always going to be with you!" Then it struck me. "You were raped, Lance. Maybe not physically, but you were raped tonight and it's my fault."

"Why do you say that? How can it be your fault?"

"Because we've been so up front with Mama, so lax with the family. People found out about us because of Rick, you know. I should have kept our secret from Rita and Trinket."

"How, Angel? I'd be down the hall, and you'd have to sneak in and out of my bed."

He was smiling a little now, and that made me smile, too. "I snuck into Uncle Sean's window one night and slept in his bed, so I could have done the same thing with you."

Lance shook his head. "Rita would still know, Will. She's smart. I'll just bet if we knew the truth, she's figured out about May, too."

Later, I had to get another look at the cut I'd seen, but I still didn't want to alarm Lance—or let him know it looked like a knife cut. I didn't even want to think someone was actually intent on castrating him. So when we had brushed our teeth and were back in our room, naked, I left the light on and laid him on the bed; I kissed him on the stomach then slid farther down, kissing and inspecting him, saying, "Nope, nobody bruised you here..." Kiss. "...or here..." I moved farther down until I was at eye-level with his balls. I glanced up at his face. He was sprawled out, arms flung above his head, eyes closed, enjoying my kisses.

He had an erection, and I caressed it, then cupping his balls in my hands, I lifted them with my eyes inches from the cut. He moaned softly, so I studied the wound. Sure enough, it was a straight, thin line, and I almost cried out in anger. Instead, I gently licked the wound and was glad he didn't say it hurt. He just moaned with pleasure.

Still later, when we were lying skin to skin, both with stiff-ons, I said, "you're really not too hurt?"

He kissed me on the mouth. "I will be if you don't make love to me."

I felt my little buddy throb at that. We were both emotionally strung out and clung to each other with the same desperation our love had always brought on. Lance had been abused all his life, had been forced at the hands of his stepfather and, tonight, at the hands of strangers, to submit his body. Even in our own love-making he always took me inside him, making me—for all the stupid guys who can't imagine otherwise—the man, making him the woman. I'd never thought about it like that, but that's how his attackers thought of him. Now he was wrapped in my arms, the smaller of the two of us, and I felt his warmth as he snuggled into my chest. It wouldn't be long before we made love. We couldn't lie next to each other in bed for long without making love. And when he sat up to get a little glycerin and rosewater on his fingers, I caught his hand in the dark. "Tonight," I said, lying back and pulling him on top of me, "I want you inside me."

He gasped. "Really? I...I've never done that." His voice was a whisper, with a slight, deep-throated quality. "Are you sure?"

I kissed him in response. "Umhmm. I want to feel you inside me. I want my man to make love to me."

Later, after he had put the lotion on his fingers and sent me to the moon with what he was doing down there, he entered me. At first, I was afraid he was too big, afraid it was going to hurt or tear. But he got me so hot with his finger, his lips on mine, the heat of his own little buddy pressed against me, that when he slid into me, I threw my legs over his shoulders, and met his pounding hips with thrusts of my own. We were in sync so much, experiencing a new act of lovemaking, I couldn't get him deep enough and cried out for him to bury it.

He went wild, was all over me with his lips and his hands, and I held him by the hips and the flesh of his butt. We were both crying, and our tears slicked our faces. When he was done, I wouldn't let him pull out, couldn't let him go, and he fell onto me breathing heavily. I couldn't imagine loving him more deeply than at that moment.

"Thank you, Angel. Thank you. I've never done that. It…it makes me feel…"

We fell asleep like that, then woke up in the middle of the night and did it again. Even though I was a little sore, it wasn't long before I was into it, again, amazed at how wild it felt.

* * *

And so here I am at close to four in the morning, hard as a rock remembering Lance inside me and trying to make sense of how good and natural our love is—even if others hate us for it.

Now I see what Uncle Sean was trying to protect me from, when he said how Theodore Seabrook was murdered. I'm grateful Lance escaped being raped—or worse. How close Lance had come to being castrated tonight made me shake, even thinking of it. I know that Uncle Sean must have been crazy with grief and hatred, how it must have drove him insane to lose the love of his life. Which made me admire him all the more for how he got on with things, afterward.

First chance I got this weekend, I would call and ask his advice about what I should do about Lance's attackers.

# Five
# Something About Casey

It's been two weeks since I've had a chance to write in this notebook. It was the very next Monday after the game, however, that I caught Casey off by himself at school. It was lunch time, and Lance was going to be busy with the Barker twins on some art project, so I was just having a Coke and candy bar out back of the school. A few of the guys who smoke were gathered there too, sending up smoke into the clear fall air. Casey had seen me before I saw him, and he was trying to get into the school building before I spotted him.

When our eyes met, I saw the same fear I'd seen that night in the hallway, and I knew he was afraid of me. That was fine, but his look also meant he knew something I wasn't going to like. He looked like a rabbit, just then, about to have his brains blown out with nowhere to run. But I give him this: when he knew I'd seen him, he looked around and came up to me. We walked off to an empty spot out of earshot of the others.

"You gotta know, Will," he said, still looking frightened, "I didn't have nothin' to do with the other night."

"You just happened to be there. Is that it?" I was mad and wanted to slam him against the building. "After all, Casey, you egged on Dick and some of the other guys about me and Lance. Ain't that right?"

He looked me straight in the eyes, and it was odd, it was the first time I noticed, really, that he wasn't a bad looking guy. He's what Daddy would have called 'black' German. Until then I'd never thought about what he meant. I'd always thought of Germans as being blond. I knew the Zumwalt family was German, though, and never thought more about it than that. But as Casey looked at me, I noticed that his eyes were black as coals. His eyebrows were dark, almost black, and his hair was a dark brown. Anyway, he looked me straight in the eyes, then looked away.

"Yeah. All right, so I was having a little fun. And it was wrong to spread the rumors. But I heard it from Rick."

In there somewhere was an apology, but it still made me want to slug him, because I saw he was kind of a coward, not willing to take any of the blame, which is probably why whatever he saw that night in the girls' locker room scared him. "That ain't no damn excuse to go around trying to ruin a guy's reputation, Casey. Lance says he almost got raped."

"I know," Casey said. "Which is why I told Coach Grey what was going down. Then I went looking for you, 'cause Coach acted like I was talking Greek. Only I guess he went into the girls' locker room, anyway, 'cause when you got there, I saw those guys were gone."

"You went back?" I asked, feeling a little better.

"I followed you, Will. Only I was afraid to go in there, afraid of what they might've done."

"But you were there, weren't you, when those guys were about to rape Lance?"

Casey looked back into my eyes, shaking his head. "They weren't planning on raping him, Will. Geez! They were serious, man. They were going to cut his nuts off! That's when I got outta there and went looking for help."

I shivered, even though it was a bright, warm day for early fall. "So you know who it was, don't you?"

He nodded and told me who. I couldn't have been more wrong, and I was a little relieved that it wasn't guys from Cotton City or Animas or, apparently, other guys from Lordsburg who had been at the game. As I said before, people know strangers in the area, and Casey said he was sure it was some of the workers from Playas. Knowing this made my stomach flip over, because it meant that the guys were all adults. I couldn't help but think of Lance's stepfather. Who knew what a tight little town Playas was? Who knew how these men found out about Lance? It was easy to believe that the rumors about Lance and me had reached the town of Playas, because some of the guys who had graduated from high school in Animas had gone to work at the plant. It wouldn't be too long before people here would know most of the people there, and they sure enough would have gone to the game because we're isolated out here in the southwestern part of New Mexico. A dance, a rodeo, a football or basketball game would draw people from all over the area.

But Casey. I was sizing him up as we talked. I'd sized up all the guys I played football with, the way they played, their weaknesses and strengths, their body types, and how much heart they put into the game when it mattered. I couldn't say that I'd ever been friends with Casey, or his next older brother Stephen. I knew Rick the best, and like I said, I thought Rick was all right until I found out he'd told Margie Collins about Lance and me. Casey was the youngest of five brothers. He was also the runt of the family, in that he was just a little taller than Lance and just a little better built. Stephen had a short, compact, hog body in comparison to Casey, and Rick was tall and muscular, like his two older brothers. They had all played football, and I just bet Casey felt he had to go along with the tradition.

The fear was gone from Casey's eyes. Even though what we were talking about wasn't pleasant, he was kind of smiling at me, now that he knew I wasn't going to rip his head off.

"Look, Will," Casey said, after we tried to put names to the guys he'd seen in the girls' locker room. "I'm sorry I ever repeated anything my brother said. I'm sorry I brought on any problems for you or Lance."

I couldn't tell him it was all right, because I was still angry. But I softened a little at his genuine apology. "Well, it hurt him, didn't it?" I said. "And Dick threw the game, you know, because he didn't wanna get 'faggot sweat' on the football."

"I'll talk to Dick about that, Will. I'm sorry about that, too."

"Yeah, well, it sure was a stupid thing for Dick to do. We didn't have to lose to Lordsburg. It sure made them think they were hot stuff."

Then Casey got this quizzical look on his face, glancing at me then looking around, as if he was going to tell me a secret. "Is it, though?"

"Is it what?"

"You know. True, then?"

I knew what he was asking, but I wasn't about to tell him anything he could take to his brothers. After Friday night, I had learned a lesson. It might've been too late to put the genie back in the bottle because of the way I'd been up front with Mama and the family, but if Casey wasn't sure about Lance and me by now, I wasn't going to confirm it. It was just too dangerous. So I grinned at him, and he grinned back, making him look a lot better. "I've always heard that queers were sissies and would rather be women. Do I look like I wanna be a girl, Casey?"

He shook his head. It was odd, but he looked disappointed about something. "No, you sure aren't." Then he worked his left shoulder and rubbed it with his right hand, as if he were injured. "The way you knocked me around that day during practice, I know you're not a sissy. You're more like a locomotive."

"Then I don't see how I could be a faggot, either, do you?" I didn't like being dishonest, but it was more important to protect Lance from the bullies and the bad guys than it was to shove my being gay down anybody's unwilling throat. It had almost got Lance castrated. It wasn't going to happen again.

Casey just shook his head, again, at my question and still looked disappointed when the bell rang and we parted.

* * *

My next target was Dick Lamb. Only I didn't try to get him alone, remembering the way he'd made his accusations in front of the other guys that time in the locker room a couple of years before. It was easy to put him in his place back then, but he'd been emboldened by the rumors and the apparent approval he got from the likes of Casey Zumwalt. So I caught him in the hallway between classes and began by slamming him into his locker and knocking his books to the floor. People stopped in mid-stride. Conversations came to a screeching halt. Girls got frightened looks on their faces, like they always do when two guys get into it at school.

Dick's fists came up fast, but I could tell from the look in his eyes that his heart wasn't in getting into a fist fight, so I knocked them away.

"Hey, what's with you, Will!" Dick said, as if he didn't know.

If I had really been out-of-control-angry, I might have begun screaming, but it was more like an act I had to go through. "First, Dick-head, next time you throw a game because you think I'm a faggot, I'm going to beat you to a pulp, and then see who's the bigger man."

I heard gasps around me, because I had said it loud enough for anybody to hear. I saw Coach Grey coming down the hall at a fast walk. He was the only teacher in the hall at the moment, and I was glad it was him, because he needed to see I was going to fight back, too, and not take the rumors anymore.

"Everybody says you are!" Dick said. His chest was heaving, so I knew he was either mad or scared. He was pretty big, but I knew I could take him in a fight.

"'Everybody' is just you and a couple of other guys, Dick-head. And second, you almost got Lance hurt real bad. He saw you the other night before he was jumped. You were in on it, weren't you—you and half a dozen grown men, picking on a single guy?"

I didn't think too many people knew about what had happened, and I saw confusion on the faces of some of the other students, but they were quickly moving out of the way as Grey plowed through them to get to me.

"It wasn't me!" Dick said.

"But you were there! You and—"

"Enough!" Coach Grey said, grabbing my arm and spinning me away from Dick. "Both of you! Right now! In my office!"

Dick picked up his books, while Coach waited, and then we both followed him to his office, which was right next to the gym.

Grey, like almost every other teacher at school, ran a small ranch or was into farming. And he was as strong as a bull and about as tall as I was. My stomach was doing a number, and I felt a little sick. At least I'd find out what he knew and what he thought. When we got to his office, and he held the door open for us, I shoved Dick hard enough that he almost tripped.

"I said enough, Will!" Coach growled behind me as he shut the door. "You two want to fight, take it off campus."

Coach sat on the edge of his desk and made us sit in front of him. Dick was still stunned and was breathing heavy. I felt angry, but at least I'd gotten things out front. So before Coach had a chance to speak, I said, "Dick was in on that trouble Lance had the other night, Coach. Lance saw him. Casey says those guys were planning to castrate Lance."

Coach just shook his head, and I didn't know if he was denying what I said or thought it was terrible. He was about as old as Daddy was, but didn't look nearly as worn out, so I figured he just ran a few head of cattle for a little extra income, and probably hired cowboys to do the real work.

"It was a bad business, Will," Coach said. "I'll give you that. But Dick wasn't there."

"Then tell me who was," I said, "and I'll kill every one of them."

"You're not going to do no such thing. My bet is they were from over at Playas. You ask me, they're just a bunch of riffraff, moving in here for the work. They'll be gone as soon as the plant's finished."

"They should be arrested and thrown in jail," I said back.

Dick looked back and forth between Coach and me, his eyes growing wider. I think he realized the same thing Casey had, that Lance could have really been hurt, and I don't think he ever meant for his own stupidity to go as far as it had.

"I've already reported the incident to the state police. They're going to patrol the next game, because the last thing we need here is to have out-of-towners disrupt our functions or hurt one of our students."

Then Coach's eyes met mine, and I saw he was angry, as well, and maybe a little curious, but he wasn't about to ask me. I appreciated that, but I had to have my say, now that I saw he wasn't a lunatic.

"Dick blew the game, Coach, all because he thought I'm queer! Just because Lance is living with my family, and just because Dick has 'faggot' on the brain, Lance almost got hurt bad."

Coach was not stupid, and I knew he knew what went on in the showers and heard all the sex talk among the guys, but until now nothing had come of it. That is, until Rick Zumwalt had begun talking, and who knew who else. I doubted that Grey heard much of that or didn't listen to it if he did.

"You did blow the game," Coach said, turning to Dick. "You're not the only quarterback material we have at this school, and if you can't distinguish between rumors and fact, then I'll start Ty or Dave next week. You got that?"

Dick just ducked his head and mumbled that he did.

Then Coach looked at me with distaste. "I have to give you this, Will, you're so confident of your manhood you didn't get too upset with all the rumors about you and that new kid, but you should have been upset long before now. It's just about the filthiest thing I can think of to be one of them Nancy boys." Then he looked at Dick, leaving me feeling like a squashed bug. "I've had enough of this kind of talk. You understand?"

Dick nodded, glancing at me kind of sheepishly, I thought. I didn't know what to make of it, like if he was sorry or something, or cowed by the coach. I felt angry with the coach, though, because of his remark. Then we both looked at the coach.

"It's plain impossible for Will to be a queer," Coach said to Dick. "Look at him! Any man'd be proud to have him as a son, and he's doing that poor Surfett kid a favor taking him under his wing. Kid's had a hard life from what I hear, so you just cool it about all this queer business, and let's get back to being the tight team we've always been."

As we were leaving Coach's office, I had a really bad feeling in my gut. When I had arrived at the girls' locker room the other night, nobody was there—including Coach. If he had gone in there to find out what was happening, and if he had scared off Lance's attackers, why hadn't he taken care of Lance? At that thought, I turned on my heels and walked right back into Grey's office.

"How come you didn't check on Lance, Coach, if you ran off all those other guys?"

"Shut the door," he said, looking odd as hell. His eyes narrowed as I shut it and sat down.

"So...how come, Coach?"

A window high up in the wall let in the early afternoon light behind the coach, causing a kind of halo around his thinning hair. He was still sitting on the edge of his desk. He smiled at me, though kind of sadly. "Like I said before, Will, you should've been upset weeks ago, when all the rumors started, which makes me think a kid like you—an honest kid to the bones from what I've seen—isn't going to deny something that's true."

"So you're saying you think I'm a queer, too?"

He leaned forward still smiling and still looking sad. "We go through this kind of thing every once in a while. But it's usually the sissy boys that get singled out when you kids discover homosexuality. People don't like homosexuals, Will."

I was getting annoyed quick, because Coach was talking in circles, and I was still smarting about his remark about how dirty he thought queers are, and he wasn't answering my question.

"Yeah, so I know that Coach. Dick-head has it on his brain. But what does that have to do with Lance? How come you didn't check on him?"

He shrugged. "I didn't know he was in there. Truth is, when Casey came running to me, I didn't much follow what he was saying, only that some guys were acting up in the girls' locker room. So I checked it out and nearly got knocked down. Three or four guys ran out when I opened the door. I did look around in there but didn't see anybody else."

I couldn't shake the feeling that coach was lying to me, because just a few minutes before that, he'd said he had reported the incident to the police. But I didn't feel like calling him on it. I was getting nowhere. I'd just have to keep my eyes open and listen more around school.

"And what you said about queers being the filthiest thing there is? Would you have helped Lance, if you had seen him, since you think it's so filthy?"

Coach's eyes widened with surprise at my accusation, then narrowed. "Listen to me, Will. You're one of the intelligent boys on the team. I meant it when I said any man'd be proud to have you as their son. What I said about homosexuals and being filthy—that was for Lamb's benefit." He looked over my shoulder, and I glanced behind me. The door was shut, and we were alone.

My legs were beginning to shake. "I don't understand what you're trying to tell me, Coach."

He sighed. "I'm saying you're young, and whatever you're feeling, whatever it is you're experimenting with, it's just a phase lots of boys go through." Then he leaned back, looking pleased with himself. "You've just gone through a traumatic time in your life with the death of your father. I'd say in a few years when you look back on all this, you'll realize the truth of what I'm telling you."

I didn't know what to say. My ears burned realizing Coach thought I was having sex with Lance, but he was brushing it off, saying what I felt for him was just some counterfeit thing. I got up then, mumbled "thanks," and was about to open the door and leave, but Coach stood up from the desk and put his hand on my shoulder.

"Look, Will. I shouldn't be having this conversation with you. The truth is, I don't think homosexuality is healthy. But boys are curious, and farm boys take opportunities with livestock you probably already know about. But it's just a phase they go through when they're curious about sex."

I got a sick feeling down in my chest at what he was implying. Though I had heard things, and it was kind of a joke among my friends about sheep, it made me so angry that he was even thinking to compare what Lance and I had with some horny kid experimenting with a milk cow or something.

"Well, I'm not experimenting, Coach!" I said it with as much calm as I could, but my voice quivered. All I wanted to do was slug him.

He nodded. "All right. Have it your way, Will. Just don't be surprised when people are disgusted by such as this. Or if you end up getting hurt."

My face stung with embarrassment and I could feel the blood rush to my cheeks, but my anger had subsided a little. Coach wasn't trying to be hateful, even though he'd insulted me. When the bell rang for the start of the next class, I took the opportunity to leave his office quickly.

In a way, Coach was just like Casey and the others. He couldn't believe I could really be gay, even if he thought I was having sex with another boy. So again, I realized it was kind of easy to lie to people like him, a boy like me, an athlete, because he didn't know the first thing about being queer. This was the way out of the mess I'd put Lance in. Just let them think I wasn't queer because I wasn't a sissy.

It was so easy, it made me laugh, and when I met Lance shortly after that, I felt like kissing him right there in the hall. If someone freaked, I'd just tell them I was curious and it wasn't something I'd be doing the rest of my life. Then I laughed again and threw my arm around Lance and walked down the hall like that until I realized he was embarrassed.

It might still take time for things to die down, but with Dick and Casey off our backs, I figured the bad part was over. I just needed to watch out for Lance.

# Part Two
# Changes

## Six
## The Harvest

It turned out I was right. I think the rumors died down, because people just didn't see how I could be queer—especially because of how "upset I was that day I attacked Dick Lamb in the hallway. Also, since Lance was my friend, I guess they didn't figure he could be queer, either. I let them believe their cock-eyed notions that queers were guys who really wanted to be girls and all that kind of bull. So, at school, things went on as usual. We heard occasional remarks about us being queer. But the neat thing was, now, Dick or Casey, or some other guy on the football team, would defend us and tell the other person to shut up, or go "f" themselves. So it was only during football games that the rumors resurfaced, when guys from the other teams would shoot off their mouths in the line, and we'd all hit back harder. Our team began to stomp the competition, as we usually did. I didn't like living a lie, but I didn't want Lance to suffer any more. He soon began to brighten back up and to enjoy school again.

So in private, we made love more than ever. I enjoyed taking him inside me as much as the other way around, and I think it was one of those things that made him feel even better about himself. When we were working in the field—by now, mainly cleaning up the weeds going to seed and piling up the masses of Russian Thistle (tumbleweeds) and burning them—Lance taught me another kind of love making, what he called "sixty-nine." It drove me crazy, because we could be out in the open, alone, and we'd be making out when we were taking a break, and things would get heavy. Then we'd get naked and lay out our clothes right there under the wide blue sky and go face-to-crotch. It was like tasting some delicious meal, the way we gobbled each other's little buddies. Then we'd turn when we both finished and smash our lips together.

Then came the weekend when Mr. Trujillo came to the farm to thresh the grain. I hired Casey and Dick to help us sack it up, showing them the twine and the "needles" we used to tie up the sacks, how the grain would collect in the hopper, how to attach the sack, then how to open the hopper until the sack was full.

It was a beautiful fall day, just after the beginning of November. I'd been kind of worried we would have to delay the harvest because, a few days before, storm clouds had gathered in the west, black and menacing underlit by the sun from the east. But the clouds just burned out, and when Trujillo's trucks pulled into the farm from the north just after sunup, it was all business. Casey and Dick tried to pitch in unchaining the tractor from the trailers, but Trujillo seemed annoyed and told them to stand back. He had brought a crew of three other men, besides himself. Men I didn't recognize, only they weren't too friendly and didn't speak English very well. So the four of us, me and Lance and Casey and Dick, stood off to the side on the edge of the field until the combine was connected to the tractor.

Mama and Trinket came out to watch. May was off with her friend Kelsey that weekend, and she had seemed happy to be out of there for awhile. I didn't know where they were planning to go, except they packed food in a cooler and tossed hiking boots and sleeping bags into the back of Kelsey's pickup. Rita didn't bother to come out of the house, so I figured she had got in late the night before.

A slight breeze came up from the north, bringing a refreshing coolness to the day. It wouldn't last, though; later, it would be hot and we'd be sweating and itching from the chaff finding its way down our shirt collars. The only one I was really worried wouldn't be able to keep up with the work was Lance, not because he wasn't strong enough, but because he hadn't spent his life on a farm. So far, he hadn't spent a sixteen-hour day doing back-cracking labor. We would work at a killer pace to finish in one day. Casey knew the routine, and Dick was strong enough to lug the full grain sacks from beneath the hopper and begin stacking them on the platform where Casey and Lance were to sew them shut. When we had a good stack of bagged grain, Dick tossed the sacks to me across the gap between the combine and the trailer and I stacked them on the far end. We had plenty of muscle power, so the work went swiftly. By the time we broke for lunch around one o'clock, one trailer was full.

I watched Lance working. He turned out to be the best at sewing up the sacks with the thick twine. The first few that Casey had done were too full of gaps and some of the golden-orange grain spilled out onto the ground when Dick tossed the sacks to me on the trailer.

Trujillo drove the pickup and went for supplies at the head of the field when they were running low. He brought us water in a plastic, gallon jug, which we passed around about once every half hour. The jug soon became streaked with sweat and dirt, and Casey was the only one who wiped off the mouth when it was passed to him. The water was like not tasting anything at all, as hot as we were, but it washed the grit down our throats.

After lunch we worked well into the afternoon, and when the sun slipped behind the Peloncillo Mountains in the west, we flipped on the flood lights on the tractor, the combine, and the pickup and kept working. Not once had Lance complained. The three Mexicans working for Trujillo talked only among themselves. At first they had talked and laughed as they worked, but as the day had dragged on, they just passed grunts back and forth.

Something about working alongside Dick and Casey, all of us sweating like pigs, feeling the same aches in our shoulders, our eyes all lined with rings of sweat and dirt, sometimes knocking our shoulders together—all this brought the four of us closer together. Sometimes, Lance and Casey (the two smallest guys) relieved me or Dick in moving the bags of grain. And when Lance slipped backward, almost falling between the combine and the trailer, Casey caught him in his arms and struggled to keep from falling himself. The way they had to entwine their arms to get back into place, the closeness of their tired and sweaty bodies, each helping the other, gave me an image of how maybe Lance and I looked together, and it was a neat image. But when I imagined Casey and Lance crossing that line and kissing, as Lance and I always did, I was disturbed. I didn't ever want to see that.

We finally came to the last row and everybody cheered at the same time. Just another half-hour and we'd be done. I had no idea what time it was, nor had I kept count of the bags of grain we'd harvested, but I thought Daddy would be proud to see that year's harvest of grain sitting on our two flat-bed trailers under the flood lights, rows and rows of bags, seven bags high. But it was also a first for us on the Barnett farm, because in years past, we'd just let the grain be threshed into a sided trailer owned by Mr. Hill. He'd pay Daddy an agreed-upon amount and just truck the grain to his silos.

The four of us saw Trujillo and his crew off that night. He said he'd be back the next day to get his equipment and to settle up. I was too tired to think about it, though, so I just shook his hand and thanked him for the work.

Mama had supper waiting for us, even though it was near ten o'clock by the time we had all showered, our filthy clothes shaken out and put in the washer, and all of us dressed again.

I'd never had friends sleep over, because Daddy always said he couldn't see putting Mama to all the trouble and switching beds and such. But Casey and Dick needed to sleep over tonight, because tomorrow, as soon as the sun came up, we had to pull the trailers with the grain out of the field and load it into the barn.

Rick dropped Rita off and came into the house for just a minute to say hello to Mama. He looked surprised when he saw his younger brother and Dick at the dinner table.

"They helped me harvest the grain," I said, explaining their presence. "And they're working for me tomorrow."

Rick did his lopsided grin thing, but there was a nasty glint in his eyes when he glanced at Casey, which made Casey drop his eyes for a second. I wondered what that was all about, but I didn't think I really wanted to know. I figured Rick might have been disappointed that Casey and I were now friendly with each other.

I was relieved when he pecked Rita on the cheek and left.

Since May was on her camp-out with Kelsey, I thought I'd have a little fun with Casey and Dick. I could've made up the couch for one of them to sleep on, but I didn't. So after we'd done the dishes and seen Mama off to bed, I led Dick and Casey into

May's room and showed them the double bed. I could see a kind of stricken look on Dick's tired face, but Casey raised his eyebrows as he looked at the bed, then at Dick. Whatever that look was, it was gone in an instant as he glanced at me and lowered his eyes.

"You boys don't do anything I wouldn't do," I teased, pulling back the covers and getting an extra pillow out of May's closet, up where Uncle Sean used to keep that box of his with the books and Theodore Seabrook's dog tags.

Both Dick and Casey glared at me, and I just grinned. "Don't be so nervous, girls. It's just for one night."

* * *

Despite all our aches and pains and being dog tired, Lance and I got naked and made slow, lazy love, falling asleep with our faces and breath sharing the same pillow.

# Seven
# Attempted Thievery

"You boys sleep all right?" Mama asked as Casey and Dick made it into the kitchen and sat down at the table.

I noticed Dick's face go red at Mama's question. When I looked over at Casey, he was trying to wipe a grin off his face. Our eyes met, and there were questions in his. Lance was sitting to my right, and I heard him say "hmmm" under his breath. I think we were thinking the same thing. I doubted if I could get anything out of Dick, but I figured Casey was open to a discussion, as long as I didn't freak him out by coming on too direct.

I remembered the day I had cornered him outside school, asking him about what had happened in the girls' locker room after the game, and he had tried to get me to tell him if it was true about Lance and me. He had looked disappointed when I denied it. Now it made sense. Even though he had been one of our persecutors, there was something under the surface, just like there was with Dick that told me things.

I figured if a guy was too conscious or curious about who was queer and who wasn't, it was because he thought about it a lot. Maybe, if Lance and I were going to be friends with Dick and Casey, we'd all be able to talk things out. I really had no idea if they had done more than just fall into bed and sleep like the dead. I know that Lance and I fell asleep in the middle of love making the night before.

Still…I watched them sitting side by side, eating their eggs and pancakes, making appreciative noises at Mama. Trinket came in when we were all about to finish and said hello as if there was nothing unusual about Casey and Dick being there. Then Rita came in, poured herself a cup of coffee and mumbled hi and asked me if we'd finished the harvest. Our eyes met, too, and again, there was something in them, but not the smirky annoyance Rick had shown the night before. Only Rita didn't look too happy this morning. I hoped she and Rick hadn't had a fight about something. But I didn't have time to dig, especially with Dick and Casey here. I made a note to talk to Rita later on.

Just about an hour after sunup, when the four of us were hooking one of the trailers up to the pickup and the other one to a tractor, Trujillo and his crew came barreling down the road, turning into the farm and heading down the field road toward us. A couple of minutes later, they pulled up in a cloud of dust. Trujillo was in his Dodge pickup, and the crew pulled up in a semi-tractor rig they would load the equipment on.

The crew didn't waste any time starting up the motor on the tractor-combine and letting down the lift to drive it onto the trailer. But Trujillo just stood by his pickup for a minute puffing on a cigarette, looking around at the now barren stalks of grain and off into the clear blue of the morning. After a while he sauntered up to where I was about to get into the cab of the pickup.

Mr. Trujillo was about as old as Daddy, somewhere in his fifties. I knew he never had any sons, and I think he only had a daughter who was off somewhere, about as old as my oldest sister Julianne.

"Mornin' Mr. Trujillo," I said, when he came up to me, squinting at me and my friends. "Thanks again for helping with the harvest. Daddy always depended on you, and I can see why."

He just grunted, cocking his hat back on his head. "Your father. He always paid me in cash, eh? This hundred-mile round trip to harvest your forty acres of grain is a pain in the ass. Es expensive, no?"

"I guess so, Mr. Trujillo. You said you'd have to charge a little more this year, on account of the diesel prices."

"Leetle bit, eh?" he said, making a small space between thumb and forefinger. "I figure with diesel, wear on the equipment, pay for the crew, time to drive out here for your little forty acres, I'll settle for fifteen hundred. Cash."

I felt like I'd been slugged in the stomach. "Daddy never paid you more than six hundred, Mr. Trujillo. Ain't that pretty good pay for a day's work?" I was about to panic, because if I sold the whole lot of grain tomorrow, it'd only bring about two thousand to twenty-five hundred.

"Look, see," he said, putting his hand on my shoulder. I felt like shaking it off. "Ef not for me, your grain, it just lay here and ruin, eh? Now what good es dat?" He took his hand off my shoulder and brought both of his hands palm up.

I noticed his Mexican accent had got a little more thick, his voice a little more gruff.

"I might as well have just let it rot in the field, Mr. Trujillo. Fifteen hundred is plain robbery and you know it."

That's when Lance must have seen the stricken and angry look on my face. He and Casey and Dick had been standing off by one of the trailers, ready to start rolling the trailer to the barn, but he said something to Casey and came over to me and Mr. Trujillo.

Trujillo glanced his way, then turned to his crew and said something in Spanish. Then he looked right at me. "Jur leetle wifey boy here. I suggest he go on now."

"It's all right," I said to Lance. "You guys go on and take that first trailer to the barn."

But Lance didn't move. He'd heard enough to know I was having trouble. And he sure heard the insult Trujillo had just made to my face about him.

I shook my head. It was like a dream, and everything began to slow down. I saw Casey and Dick exchange looks and begin moving slowly toward me, as if they were trudging through molasses. I saw the puffs of dust explode from under their boots.

Then, as if it was magnified in the still air, I heard the unmistakable Ka-chink, ka-chink of the shotguns two of Trujillo's crew suddenly had in their hands as they pumped shells into the chambers, leveling them in slow motion on Casey and Dick. They saw them at the same time, coming to an exaggerated stop, first one foot, then the other, their faces grimacing in fright and confusion.

"No trouble, eh?" Trujillo was saying to me, as I came back to reality. I was so angry I could feel my legs beginning to shake. Trujillo had planned on this robbery. And that's exactly what it was, pure and simple. His eyes told me he knew it, as we faced off.

"What're you going to do, Mr. Trujillo? Kill all of us and steal the grain? You think you won't get your thieving ass thrown in jail? Then what good is your fifteen hundred gonna do? Maybe you thought you could scare me into paying you?"

He blinked and waved angrily at his crew, and that's when I knew he hadn't counted on me calling his bluff. They lowered their shotguns.

Dick and Casey stood as still as statues, like in that game, frozen in the same position they had landed in when they were tagged.

I took my eyes off Trujillo and turned to Lance. His face was ashen, and fear flooded his eyes. "Lance. You, Casey, and Dick go on, now. Drive the trailers to the barn. Me and Mr. Trujillo have to settle up."

Lance looked doubtful, but I tried a smile. "It's all right!"

When Lance got in the pickup and started it up, I stepped out of the way, walking straight at Mr. Trujillo, forcing him to step back. I was taller and bigger than he was. Still, he moved back reluctantly. Casey loped to the tractor with Dick on his heels, and when Casey started up the tractor and followed Lance in the pickup, I was alone in the field with Mr.

Trujillo and his crew. "I'll negotiate with you Mr. Trujillo, but I sure as hell won't be robbed."

"Hey! Hey! Just a little test, boy!" he said, in completely unaccented English.

I thought better of telling him I didn't appreciate his test. My stomach was in knots, and I believe if I hadn't stood up to him, he really did think he could take what he wanted. And I knew why. Like everyone else, he had heard about me and Lance and thought he was dealing with a cream-puff.

"Since diesel has doubled in the last couple of years," I said, trying to keep my voice steady, "you tell me what you think is a fair price, Mr. Trujillo, and I'll pay it."

* * *

My stomach was still in knots when I finally got home. Lance had unhooked the trailer from the pickup and came roaring back to the field about fifteen minutes after he left. I knew he was scared, just like me. But we road home in silence, and as soon as he pulled to a stop, I went into the house and asked Mama to write a check out to Mr. Trujillo for eight hundred dollars.

"My! That's an awful lot, Will. Your father felt robbed with a lot less than that."

"I know, Mama. This'll be the last time we deal with him."

* * *

All of my playfulness with Casey and Dick was gone by the time we started unloading the grain off the trailers. They were still looking frightened and angry when I told them what had happened.

"Near made me shit my goddam pants!" Dick said. "And you say he was just testing you?"

"He thought he could take advantage," I growled. "Did you hear the insult he made on me and Lance?"

"Called me Will's wifey boy," Lance said, softly.

"Oh," Casey said. "I guess he heard it from someone."

I felt like reminding Casey that someone would most likely be his damned brother, Rick, but decided against it.

We were all sweating like pigs as we worked. Today, it was a lot harder to keep up the grueling pace, so we spent a lot of time sitting around on the bags of grain in the cool of the barn. After awhile, we had all calmed down. I didn't like it when Casey started calling me 'tough' man and Dick chiming in with his own praise. I was probably more scared than I had ever been in my life. It was only when I realized that Trujillo wasn't about to use the shotguns that I knew he was bluffing and trying to steal from me, hoping I was as scared as I was.

"Just don't let this go any further, guys. Okay?"

"But why, Will?" Casey said. "Guys at school will think you're really tough, now. I guarantee they'll never give another thought to…you know…"

"I know," I said. "I just don't want it to get around. It might get back to Trujillo. He's mad enough as it is. I think he really thought he was going to walk away with all that money."

He and Dick were sitting side-by-side on a stack of grain, and even though I never did think Dick was all that good looking, I smiled inwardly thinking it would be neat if they were boyfriends. All around us, the odor of the grain was rich and sweet. We were sweating and our faces were streaked with grit and dirt. We were all shirtless, and our chests glistened with sweat. It was hard to believe it was November.

Lance and I were sitting even closer together on our own stack of grain bags. In fact, he was running his hand up and down my back. I enjoyed his brash act, just out of sight of Dick and Casey.

* * *

It's now Sunday afternoon. Dick and Casey left a while ago, and Lance is taking a nap. I wish I was in there with him, but I needed to write down everything that happened. I think I know, now, what gave Daddy his ulcers, why he sometimes flew off the handle and ended up slugging people, like the time he socked Old Man Hill in the face when his cattle got in our corn crop. I even understand why he was suspicious of 'book learning' and only considered a man a real man if he had a strong back and hard hands. In this part of the country, at least, I'm beginning to learn that there's always someone waiting to take advantage of you, to pounce like a cat on a mouse, if you show the slightest sign of weakness. It's probably that same thing that makes people out here hate boys they think are not real men, which is what they really mean by 'queer' and 'faggot.' The part about two men having sex probably doesn't really matter to them when they bother to think about it. What Coach Grey said about farm boys and their animals comes back to me now and then, and kind of makes me cringe at the thought.

Anyway, Mr. Trujillo must have been thinking I wasn't enough of a man to hold my own against him with the stunt he pulled, having his hired hands brandish those shotguns. Maybe he thought I'd run off scared and crying and let him rob me and my family blind. But I've had the farm long enough, now, to know how to protect it.

So Daddy. The more I learn things working your farm, the more I understand and admire you. The more I miss you, too!

But I've got to say this: I'm not going to let this farm eat me alive like it did Daddy. I kind of want to see what the rest of the country's like. I think when Christmas rolls around this year, I'm going to buy me and Lance a set of wedding bands. Even if we don't wear them while we're at school and just carry them around in our pockets, we'll know what it means.

# Eight
# Trouble for Casey

It's odd how the same bad things happen to different people. I'm up here in the loft of the barn. It's Monday afternoon, mid-November. Lance is off on an art field trip with Mr. Drummond and a few others from his art class. They're going up to Santa Fe to visit the art museums and to sketch northern New Mexico landscapes. They're also going to visit with that old lady painter Georgia O'Keeffe on that ranch of hers near Abiquiu. She's supposed to be famous. I don't know about that, but Lance sure was excited to go. Sleeping without him already feels empty, though.

But that's not what I meant to put down. I'm up in the barn, because I've just packed up some of my old writing, along with Uncle Sean's dog tags and that letter he wrote me a long time ago. I've sealed everything up real safe with duct tape and have stored it in the rafters. This loft is kind of a special place. It seems right that all that writing I did up here, all that learning, be stored here. Maybe one day I'll retrieve it and re-read it. But not now. So much else is going on, I need to sort through it, write it down, so I can maybe grasp what it means—like what happened to Casey Zumwalt.

The Monday after Casey and Dick helped me and Lance load the grain in the barn, Casey didn't come to school. When he did show up the next day, I saw he had been beat to a pulp—just like Lance had been when I first met him. Casey's face was bruised and his lips and eyes were swollen. It was like seeing Lance all over again, and my heart just climbed up in my throat and choked me when I saw him. Only he wouldn't talk about it and avoided everybody. He was going to suit up for practice as usual, and that's when everybody saw that someone had made hamburger out of his back, too, like he'd been whipped. Coach took one look and told him he wasn't about to get suited up. "You're in no condition to practice, Zumwalt." Then he took Casey into the locker room where he treated sprained ankles and tended bruises and smeared some powerful smelling cream on his back. That day during practice, Coach barked at us, and I could tell he was concerned about Casey.

Dick Lamb was as much at a loss as I was, so on Wednesday of that week, we decided we had to find out what happened to Casey. Only he was still evasive.

"It ain't none of you guys' damn business," he said, lowering his eyes, when I'd asked Casey who had beat him up. We were behind the high school, because Casey had avoided us in the cafeteria. I'd reluctantly told Lance I had to find out about Casey, but Lance understood. He was sympathetic to him, as well, but he looked apprehensive, himself, about something. "I have something to tell you," he said, as I was leaving to go find Casey. "But it can wait till later."

Anyway, Dick was fuming when Casey said it wasn't our business. "Geez, Casey, we're your friends! Will and I can handle whoever did this. It won't happen again, once we get through with them."

But Casey wasn't having it. Dick tried to argue with him, but Casey's swollen, red eyes pooled with tears and he turned away from us, even shaking off the hand Dick tried to lay on his shoulder, and hoofed it back into the school building.

So I was stumped and tried to quit thinking about it. Besides, that evening after practice, which Casey still didn't suit up for, I had to find out what was bothering Lance. It turned out it wasn't what he wanted to tell me that was bothering him, but his fear of telling me. So when we got into the pickup and were heading out of the parking lot, Lance still looked fearful and was quiet, rather than laughing and sitting close to me once we were out of sight of the school.

"You know you can tell me anything, Lance. You're scaring me, you know? Why are you afraid?"

This late in November, the sun was almost down as we headed east out of Animas. I glanced into Lance's beautiful face and met his shadowed eyes. I bet they were almost brown, though, because of his mood.

I put my arm around his shoulders and tried to draw him close, only he resisted for a moment; then he kind of allowed me to pull him to me.

"You won't be mad, Angel?"

"I promise. Now, please, spill it."

He told me about the trip that Mr. Drummond wanted to take his best students on to northern New

Mexico, to paint and meet that famous artist. He said it in a rush, as if saying it fast, it wouldn't be as bad. "So what d'you think? I won't go if it bothers you," he said, finally, and so nervous I could feel his heart beating as if it were my own.

I squeezed him to me. "I think it's really great, Lance. Why were you afraid to tell me?"

I felt him shrug. "Don't know. I just thought…"

"What?"

"That you wouldn't like it."

"But you're a great artist! And if you say this old lady is so world famous, and she's nice enough to show you guys around, why shouldn't you go?"

Lance sat up and scooted the rest of the way against my body and, just as we were passing the road that went off toward Playas, where lights were already shining against the jagged silhouette of the close mountain behind it, he slobbered on my cheek and ran his tongue in my ear, which always caused me to shiver with the chills. "My stepfather always made fun of my art and tore up the things he saw I was most proud of."

"But you don't think I'm like him, do you?" I was a little hurt. "C'mon, baby. Please don't even put me in the same thought with him. Okay?"

"You meant it, though? You really don't mind?" His voice already had an edge of excitement, now that he knew I wasn't going to be upset.

"As long as you paint me nude against the Sangre de Cristo Mountains or something."

He snorted a short laugh and snuggled against me.

A little while later we passed through Hachita then turned south, and it struck me. "It'll be the first time we haven't slept together since we met. You say you leave this coming Sunday and won't be back until—"

"Wednesday."

"Then we better get home and make up for all those days and nights."

* * *

It was the same thing on Thursday. Casey wouldn't talk. He looked afraid to even be seen with us, and that made me wonder what it could be. Something had spooked him, and it was breaking my heart, now that he and Dick had come over to my side about the queer business and were two of my best supporters.

We had a game on Friday night, but Casey didn't show up and, afterwards, Dick got me aside and said he was getting worried. "I ain't ever seen Casey so shook, Will. You sure you don't know at least something?"

I didn't, and I said so. "Let's just give him a little time. Maybe Monday."

So when Monday rolled around, we tried to talk to Casey. The air that morning was noticeably cooler than it had been and Casey was wearing a hooded wind breaker, pulled tight around his face. It was bright, though, and in the sunlight of that early morning before classes started, the bruises looked worse, even though I was sure they were less painful. I was relieved when he agreed to tell us what happened.

"Only let me talk to Will, first," he said to Dick.

Dick looked hurt. "What d'you mean, Casey? I thought you and me was best friends!"

Casey looked pitiful when tears kind of glistened in his eyes and he shrugged. "I will tell you, Dick. Just let me talk to Will about it first."

Dick still didn't like it, but I could tell he was as much hurt for his friend as he was for himself.

As I mentioned before, Casey was kind of the runt of his family and, in a way, that also reminded me of Lance. Some big lug of a bully must've found him easy to pick on, maybe, and I kind of felt ashamed of the way I had knocked him around during practice that one time.

So, anyway, Casey and I headed off campus to the other side of the football stadium. I sat down, leaning up against the chain-link fence. Only Casey couldn't lean back against it because his back must've still been too tender, so he just sat on the grass and hugged his knees and rested his chin on them. That also reminded me of the first time I'd laid eyes on Lance, and I recalled how I had put my arm around him and how he had just leaned into me. But I didn't think Casey would take it the right way, so I just waited for him to start talking.

When his brother Rick had told his family about me and Lance sharing a bedroom, Casey said he was surprised how upset and hateful his entire family got, his father saying I ought to be horsewhipped. "But it was Rick who got the most upset," he said, "and he told me I needed to find out for sure if you and Lance were, like, really queers."

Since I never had brothers, I didn't know about things that could go on among them, things that they might do to each other. In Casey's family, though, Casey admitted that his older brothers had always picked on him, called him a baby and a sissy if he couldn't do what they did. "They put me on a steer when I was just five or six," he said, "and when it threw me off and I broke my arm and cried about it, they teased me for weeks."

"So you just toughed your way through? Even when you were afraid or got hurt doing things?"

"Pretty much. They used to throw me off the barn and one of my other big brothers would catch me. They'd do it until I didn't scream or cry."

Geez, I thought to myself, glancing at him, his wrecked face, his wiry build. No wonder he was as tough as he was.

"But why was Rick so upset about me and Lance? What in the world makes your family so concerned if I might be queer? It sounds like you eat rocks for breakfast, because cereal is too soft."

Casey laughed at that. Then he looked me square in the eyes. His were still a little puffy and still ringed with black bruises. "They did other things to me, Will."

I didn't have to ask, because I already suspected what he meant—except I wanted Casey to tell me it wasn't that. "What do you mean?" I asked him. "What sort of things?"

He began to cry, burying his face into his knees. Then all of a sudden, he just stopped, though his chest was still heaving. He looked up at me. I was sitting on his right.

"Exactly what you're thinking."

"Geez, Casey, they raped you?"

"Kind'a. Until they got to be older and one-by-one they discovered girls."

I was relieved that they had stopped. "So they're kind of ashamed of themselves," I said. "And now that Rick thinks me and Lance are honest to goodness queers?"

"Rick's worried I'll tell somebody about him and my brothers."

It was almost like a light had gone on, a thought so clear I could see it. "So it was Rick who beat you up, because he saw you over at my house, and he was afraid you had told me about him." It wasn't a question.

But Casey shook his head. "He beat me up because I stood up for you when he was going on about you and Lance and how you might infect me with your sickness. I told him you were nothing like he was making you out to be."

"And he whipped you like that on the back? Surely—"

"My father did that, Will. He saw Rick beating on me and pulled us apart, but Rick told him that I was hanging out with you and Lance. I admitted I had spent the night over there, and Rick just pounced and accused me of being queer, too. When I tried to tell Dad it wasn't like Rick said, he wouldn't listen. I'm not supposed to be seen with you, anymore, or I'll get it again."

So that was why Casey had been avoiding me and Dick. It was my turn to feel afraid. Not for myself, or even Lance, but for Casey.

"Well, maybe you shouldn't then." I was thinking of Casey's brother, Stephen, who was a senior like me. Casey was a junior. "What if Stephen sees you? Won't he tell Rick or your father?"

Lance shook his head. "I can't not be around you, Will. I...I decided I have to be honest, here. You and Lance. I know something is between you guys, even if you won't admit it." He eyed me, just then, his eyebrows raised, but I still wouldn't answer him about that.

A moment passed.

"The thing is," he continued, "even if you're not queer, I am. That's why I wanted to talk to you without Dick being around. I don't know how he would react, you know? He's the one that started in on you about being a faggot a couple of years ago. Remember? When you wore your uncle's tags?"

I just nodded, dumbstruck that Casey had just confessed to being gay. It was my turn. "Well, maybe that was a good idea to wait to tell Dick, though I guess I ought to tell you. Lance and I are sleeping together, and it's exactly what you think it is. Only I decided it isn't anybody's business. So I won't confirm people's suspicions. You saw what almost happened to Lance."

It should have been a solemn moment, but Casey was suddenly grinning from ear-to-ear. "I won't tell anyone, Will. Honest! But if you can be queer—"

"Gay," I said. "The word's gay."

He nodded, still grinning. "Yeah. Gay. Then I sure can't see anything wrong with it. It's like finally being able to talk about stuff. It's a shit-load off my mind."

"But, Casey, your brothers made you have sex with them when you were just a kid. How do you know you're really gay?" It felt weird to be asking something like that, but I thought I should, since Casey had been abused.

He shook his head again. "I've thought about that, sure. Even though I didn't like some of the things they made me do, I really got off on the others, only I never acted like I did, because I didn't want them to know."

I still couldn't imagine how someone's own family—someone's own brothers—could do that. I shook off a really ugly image of me forcing Trinket, say, to do things to me, and again, I thought of Uncle Sean when I was after him to be my boyfriend. I just had no idea back then what he found wrong with it. But hearing Casey's story made me shake my head, and I appreciated more than ever Uncle Sean's wisdom.

It was getting close to time for class, so I got up and offered him a hand, which he took. I pulled him up. "Look, Casey," I said. "I'd just love to get Rick off by himself and beat the snot out of him, and let him know what a bastard he is. It explains a lot to me. But I don't think I can because of what he might do to you."

Casey dusted the dry grass off his Levi's and looked me square in the eye, smiling oddly. His eyes were red from crying and the black of his irises seemed as dark as a coming thunderstorm. His face was a mess. "Thanks, but I don't want you in the middle with your sister dating him. Only Rita ought'a at least know. He's pretty serious about her."

What Casey said was true, and that made my guts clench, thinking about him ever making love to her, after the way he had treated his own little brother. "Geez. I hadn't thought of that. You're not saying I ought to tell Rita about him and you, though, are you?"

Casey turned away from me and we began walking back to the school. We weren't even halfway around the football field when the buzzer sounded for class. Still, we just kept walking at a leisurely pace. "Tell Rita whatever you think you should. She deserves to know."

"I will," I said. "What about you, though? You gonna tell Dick everything you told me? I've always kind of thought he was...you know...like us, only he seems too afraid of it in himself, he's always trying to find it in other guys."

"Bingo!" Casey said. I could have sworn he was walking a little lighter, as if a big weight had dropped from his shoulders, now that we'd talked. Then he started giggling. "That's what I've always thought, too, only there for awhile, you know, after Rick told us about you and Lance, I was kind of fighting it myself. I hope you don't hold that against me too much."

"I don't," I said. "How could I, considering everything you just told me?" It seemed we'd both come a long way and maybe Casey had come a lot further with all he'd had to endure. "But about Dick, though. He might be too scared if you suddenly tell him about yourself. You need to think hard about that."

He nodded. "I guess so, but I think you're right. He may be having thoughts he's not comfortable about. You sure had him freaked out when you put us in the same bed that night."

"I don't suppose anything happened then, did it?"

Casey grinned. "I think it could've, if we hadn't been so damned tired. You worked the hell out of us, you know." Casey sounded kind of angry and, for a moment, I thought he was insulted by my question.

"So you mean nothing happened?"

He grinned again. "We both crawled under the covers and just lay there on our backs, and I was drifting off when Dick rolled against me and kind of threw his leg over me. I swear he had a hard on, Will."

"And?"

He shrugged. "I woke up and it was morning! Like I said, you worked us ragged." Then he snorted. "Dick was embarrassed, though, 'cause when we woke up, we were tangled up in each other's arms. You should have seen him fly out of the bed!"

"I noticed he turned red when Mama asked you guys how you slept. But has he mentioned it?"

Casey shook his head. "Not after what happened to me. Though I think...now that you know about me and I know about you and Lance…I think I'm gonna see what he says when I tell him I'm queer."

We parted a moment later, right at the double doors at the back of the school. I'd done what I swore I wouldn't do, and that was confirm Casey's suspicions about me and Lance. Only I wasn't nervous about that, anymore. I was a little fearful that I might be wrong about Dick Lamb, and Casey just might be confessing to someone who couldn't handle it.

* * *

The ride home without Lance in the pickup was empty and lonely, but it gave me time to think about things. He'd be surprised about Casey's confession, of all people, one of our tormenters. And it felt even emptier at home with just Mama, Trinket, and Rita, and we all ate in silence, almost. It struck me deep, that if Lance hadn't come into our lives, this is what it would be like. Still, it was a good opportunity to talk to Rita about Rick. I remembered how unhappy she looked that Sunday morning when she came into the kitchen where Casey, Dick, Lance, and I were eating. What Casey said had me think hard about Rick. He was not just a jerk, but dangerous.

Rita was rarely home in the evenings because of dating Rick. But I'd noticed that she hadn't gone out for a few nights, now. So when supper was done, and she and I were doing dishes, and Mama and Trinket were in the living room, I told her I needed to talk to her. May still wasn't home from Animas, and I figured she and Kelsey were grabbing burgers or something. Only I waited until she and I had dried and put away the dishes. I sure hoped she wouldn't be too upset, because I was about to paint an ugly picture of the person she loved.

She poured herself a cup of coffee. She leaned against the counter and looked me in the eye. "So talk. You look like you're about to bust a gut." She wasn't wearing makeup that night. Now that Mama no longer bugged her about it, she didn't wear it as often, unless she was going out.

I got a cup of coffee, myself, and leaned against the counter, too.

"You know that Rick beat on Casey, right?"

She nodded and took a sip from her cup. "Oh, Will! It's just awful. The way Rick's been since he figured out about you. That's all he's been able to talk about. And when he told me he'd laid into his little brother, I was just sick. It's so hateful!"

"There's more, Rita," I said. "But I don't want you to be mad at me for telling you. Something Casey told me. He thinks you ought to know, though."

Rita turned to face me, laying a hand on my forearm. "I won't shoot the messenger, all right?"

I wasn't sure about that, but I just plowed ahead, telling her that Rick had often made Casey have sex with him. Then I said, "he was afraid Casey would tell me, or me being queer might rub off on him when he was over here."

Rita has a funny way of crying. It's silent, but it just tears me up, because she cries with her whole body, while the tears just leak out from under her lids. Luckily, there wasn't any mascara to run.

For a little while I didn't think she was going to stop crying. I had no idea what was going through her head, either. Then she sucked in her breath, a kind of high, sing-song intake. She turned her red eyes toward me, trying to smile but doing it badly. "I figured him for a bastard, once he told me how funny it was what Margie Collins did to you. He's the one who told her, you know."

"I know," I said. "Margie told me what Rick said the day she tried to get in my pants."

Rita laughed so suddenly, I did too. "I can just see her, Will! That old whore!"

"So it made you mad that he told her?"

"Of course it did! You think I want my only brother pawed by someone old enough to be our mother? I know how special you are, you and Lance. It's weird to me, though, okay? But I see how much happier you are these days, in spite of all the talk I've heard."

I told her thanks for that. I really wanted to hug her, but I felt awkward hugging anybody but Trinket. Even as close as me and May are, I rarely hug her, either.

"So what are you going to do about Rick, then? If he's that violent, he might turn on you."

She stood up to her full five feet, eight inches and took another sip of coffee, then set the cup on the counter. "I've got a lot to think about. The way Rick has been has made me cautious. Until now, though, he's never done anything to make me think he's violent."

"But what about Casey and the way Rick beat on him? And did you know Casey's father whipped him with a razor strap because Rick said he was queer like me and Lance? His back is in ribbons, Rita. If you ask me, that whole family is hateful."

We stood there side-by-side a few moments without saying anything, each of us busy with our own thoughts.

Then all of a sudden she kissed me on the cheek. "I love you, Will. Don't ever forget that, okay? If you want to know, I've been thinking about dumping Rick for quite a while. Now I have good reason."

A moment later, Rita left me in the kitchen. I looked around. I remembered when Daddy had put in the tiled counter tops. I remembered when I first saw Uncle Sean sitting at the table and how from that day I began to discover who I was. I remembered bringing Lance in here the day I found him on the rock ledge, and I could even see Daddy sitting at the head of the table, looking like he felt bad, that very same night. So much of our living was done here in this brightly lit room. It was where we had so many of our family talks.

Something passed through me, just then, as I looked around, kind of an emptiness, kind of seeing this kitchen when all of us were gone. I didn't think our family would be together much longer, and when I went to my bedroom, I was feeling kind of sad, though it wasn't the kind of feeling that brought tears to my eyes. Just a slight ache in my heart.

* * *

Which of course brings me to Lance, again. He comes back from his trip tomorrow. Mama gave him fifty dollars to spend, though the school is paying for the motels. All he has to buy is food, so he ought to be all right. I've missed him badly, and I've even played this game with myself, sitting up here in the loft, watching the sunlight fade from the Big Hatchet peak across the highway. I've been pretending that I never met Lance, to see how I feel without him. Only I can't really feel how lonely I was before he came into my life. His beauty fills my mind and wraps itself warmly around my heart.

I remember how I wrote about Uncle Sean up here, before he had ever kissed me that time in the car on the way back from Deming, and I remember how I used to get a stiff-on just picturing him and thinking my childish thoughts about what it would feel like to be naked in the bed with him. I remember calling masturbation "having a wet dream!" Tears of laughter and embarrassment spring to my eyes when I think about that, because Lance has shown me so much in the way of making love. I can remember each special moment of our love-making.

I guess the most important thing I have to tell Lance when I see him again, after I've filled his face with kisses and tell him I love him, is about Casey.

I'm depending on Lance to know how to help Casey handle things, because Lance knows what it's like to submit his body, knows what it's like to survive beatings and how to break free of the guilt and the shame. At least I think he knows these things. Maybe Lance will even know how we should be with

Casey, now that I know he's gay like we are. Hmmm. One down and one to go. Only I'm a little more nervous about admitting we're gay to Dick. But Casey promised Dick he'd talk to him. They are best friends, after all. I hope Dick won't let all that go down the toilet if Casey tells him about himself.

# Nine
# Lance Returns, and the End Begins

Oh, man! When Lance got home last night, I was waiting at the school in the parking lot, and when I saw the lights from the van as it pulled off the street, I was out of the pickup, jittery as all hell, I could hardly contain myself. It was dark, except for a few street lights in the lot and the interior lights of the van, which came on when Mr. Drummond shut off the engine and the side doors came open.

There were others waiting for the art class students, but I could hardly contain myself when I saw Lance step out onto the gravel. He'd already grabbed up his suitcase and his arms were full of things he must've got on his trip. His face was indistinct there in the light, but I knew which one was him. I just couldn't contain myself and ran up to him snatching things, saying "hi!" and "how was it?" and then I felt his hand on my chest, right there in front of everybody, running it down my shirt, and my little buddy just sprang to full attention, making a tent in my Levi's.

He hardly said bye to anybody, except Mr. Drummond, thanking him for the trip, and then we were off together, heading for the pickup, throwing his suitcase in the back, packing his bags and things under a tarpaulin I'd put in the bed of the pickup. About a second later, we were in the cab of the pickup and we just couldn't wait any longer and were smashing our faces together and hugging and feeling of each other's tents in our pants. It was lucky I'd parked a little ways off from the others.

We must've kissed for two minutes, until our faces were slick with spit, and we were both breathing heavy and had to pull apart to take a breath.

"Did'ja miss me, Angel?" Lance finally said, laughing and squeezing my little buddy.

"A little," I said, still breathing heavy. "Did you miss me?"

He kissed me on the lips and ran his tongue into my mouth. "A little," he said.

My hands were shaking with excitement as I started the engine. My vision was actually blurry I wanted to make love right then so much, I could hardly get the pickup into gear. We lurched out of the parking lot and, in a few moments, we were heading east toward Hachita. The lights of Animas were barely out of sight, when Lance began ripping at my shirt, and when it was off, he unbuckled my belt and undid the buttons on my Levi's. I tried to drive steadily, but I'm sure when he went down on me with his hot, wet mouth, and was going up and down on my already slick little buddy, I must've swerved off and onto the road. It wasn't but a few seconds before I let loose, all that pent-up desire. And then I pulled off onto the side of the road, not even bothering to check for car lights from either direction.

"In me, baby!" I whispered. "Do it in me!"

In a second I was on my back with my Levi's shoved down around my boots, and Lance flew out of his clothes. He used spit on me and worked me with his fingers, and then as slick as his own little buddy was, he slid in easily. All I felt was the heat of his naked skin against me, the hot flesh as I took him inside, and our lips and teeth, we could hardly contain ourselves.

But we weren't nearly done, and I got out of my clothes and threw them onto the floor board of the pickup with his, and as I drove, he kissed me and sucked me and ran his tongue in my ears, and we were both crying there for awhile. I couldn't believe how much a few days away from each other had brought out so much heat.

It was actually a cold night, and when we pulled into the yard at home and were dressing in the pickup, our breath showed in the air. With untucked shirts and barely buckled belts, with our arms around each other we went into the house, heading straight for our bedroom where we got undressed again and crawled naked into bed, and just fell into each other's arms and kissed long and languidly.

Lance fell asleep telling me about his trip and visiting that old lady painter. He talked about her studio and how beautiful parts of New Mexico were, and how he missed me, and had a surprise for me.

Knocking at our door around two o'clock in the morning brought me out of a deep sleep. I untangled my arms and legs from Lance, feeling suddenly chilled. I tucked the sheet and blanket around him and pulled on my Levi's. Then I padded barefoot across the floor and opened the door a crack.

It was Mama, standing there with the hall light on, smoking a cigarette, her eyes bloodshot and a shocked look on her face. Seeing her, I felt all the blood drain from my face. I stepped out into the hall, hugging myself because of the cold.

"Mama, what is it? You look bad."

"There was a phone call. I've got coffee on, Will," was all she said, as she turned with the smoke from her cigarette rising to the ceiling and led the way into the kitchen.

I was blinking in the bright lights and feeling like I was made of sand as I sat down cupping the mug of coffee in my hands. My feet felt like ice on the tile floor, so I tucked one foot under my thigh.

Mama sat down across from me. She was wearing a robe, and I could see the "v" of her chest as it disappeared beneath her robe, and I realized that her skin was kind of wrinkly, with a few freckles around her collar bone. But her face told me something was terribly wrong, the way her mouth sagged below bright, fearful eyes.

"Rita was hurt, Will, over in Cotton City, tonight. You didn't hear the phone?"

I just shook my head, trying to understand what she was saying. "How? Who did it? Who called?"

Mama told me it was Casey. Then she began to cry, though she didn't cry out, only the tears just kind of fell. And in an instant I was behind her and hugging her. She felt so bony, it shocked me. She kind of talked into my forearm, holding it with her hands. They were cold and I kept trying to hold her a little tighter. Rick was the one that beat on Rita, Mama said. And even though she didn't know why, I did. I bet she had told him it was over. So after what seemed like thirty minutes, but it was only about ten, I was dressed and out the door, again. Casey had told Mama that Rita was all right, even though Rick had started in beating on her, and she wouldn't go to the doctor over in Animas. She just wanted to come home. So I drove over there and met Casey at the Texaco out near the south edge of Cotton City.

* * *

I could have lived without Margie Collins coming over to check on Rita. But there she was bright and early the next morning while our house was in an uproar, with everybody just trying to get up and get breakfast. Mama was up and so was I, but Lance wasn't. I didn't think he ought to go to school today, and I thought I'd tell him so. May hadn't been up more than ten minutes when Mama told her what had happened to Rita, and Trinket came in crying about Rita, because she had seen her as soon as she woke up. I was just heading back to the bedroom to check on Lance when Mrs. Collins drove up. I could see who it was out the kitchen window. Geez, I thought, news sure travels fast, but then I remembered that it was Margie whom Rick went to first thing when he put two and two together and came up with me and Lance sleeping together. And she was the first person who had decided to use her calling as she had put it to cure me.

I noticed, as she walked up onto the front porch, that today her hair was red. Lucille Ball red, and about as fake and dead looking as her black hair had been. As Mama answered the door, I left for the bedroom, feeling my guts tighten up at the thought of Rita lying in her bedroom looking not quite as bad as Casey had, but because she was my sister, I felt even worse.

Lance was awake, lying in bed with only the sheet covering his naked lower torso, smiling at me when I eased open the door.

"Mornin' darlin'," he said in his best, oily New Orleans accent, and I got onto the bed with him, kissing him deeply, feeling myself go from shook-up to horny in a split second. But I resisted the temptation to go any further, and when we broke apart, I told him what had happened to Rita, and how I had gone over to Cotton City to pick her up.

He came out of his languid state as soon as he understood what I was telling him. "Is she all right?" he asked, starting to get up.

"She was a mess when I picked her up last night, but I think more angry than hurt."

Lance made it to a sitting position on the edge of the bed, but his eyes looked puffy, and I just wanted to hold him like a little kid until he woke up. I told him I thought he should stay out of school for the day, since he'd had such a long trip and, for a moment, he lay back, blinking his eyes, thinking.

"I guess I could stay around here and see if Rita needs me to help her. Shit, Will. I just hate that guy. First he rips into Casey and now Rita. I sure hope somebody lays him out. Or maybe he ought'a be thrown in jail."

I'd thought about that, and on the way home with Rita, I told her she should press charges, but she had just shaken her head in the dark, no longer crying, at least. "It's over," she said. "I just want to forget about it."

But I didn't. I wouldn't.

Lance touched me on the arm. I was sitting on the edge of the bed, kind of staring off into space, I guess.

"You're the one who ought to stay home," he said. "You've got circles under your eyes. I doubt if you can think too clearly without some sleep."

I fell back onto the bed and gathered him up in my arms and kissed him on the mouth. "I doubt I'd get any sleep, 'cause you'd be here, and I'm not finished saying welcome home yet!"

He laughed, but got up off the bed and pulled on his Levi's over his naked butt. "Let's eat. I'm starved."

That's when I told him Margie was there.

"You afraid of her?" he teased. "C'mon, Angel. Let's go give her a little thrill!"

I was dumbstruck with the thought, but grinned at him, and he winked in return.

So we went into the kitchen, barefoot and shirtless, and sure enough, Mrs. Collins stopped in mid-sentence and looked in our direction. Our eyes met, and despite my nervousness, I smirked at her and threw my arm around Lance's shoulders, feeling the warmth of his skin against my own. "Good morning, Mrs. Collins. Your new hair color is becoming."

She shot me daggers, but messed with her hair, anyway.

May sure didn't miss the exchange and when our eyes met, hers opened a little wider and she covered her mouth to hide her grin.

"But if there's anything at all I can do, Arlene, just let me know," Mrs. Collins said, after a moment, turning back to Mama.

Mama had missed the exchange between us, I guess, because she smiled at Mrs. Collins. "If you could take Trinket to the bus stop, I would appreciate it. As for Rita, I'm keeping her home from school the rest of the week."

Trinket had gotten over crying as she looked back and forth between Mama and Mrs. Collins, eating her cereal with an oversized spoon. "Can't I stay home, too, Mama?" she asked.

"No, honey. You go on now and get dressed. I'll fix you a pan of brownies when you get home."

Lance and I got our breakfast from the counter and sat at the opposite end of the table from Mrs. Collins. Out of the corner of my eyes, I saw her looking at us. The daggers were gone, but not her lust.

"So who called and told you about Rita?" I asked, before I even realized I was going to. It came out sounding accusative, and that's the way Mrs. Collins seemed to take it.

"If you must know, Will, it was Rick. He was just devastated at what happened."

Mama frowned at this, but lit a cigarette, rather than saying anything. She was upset though, because she had just put out a cigarette in the ashtray next to her coffee cup a moment before.

"Did he hurt his goddamned hand when he blackened Rita's eye?" May asked. She was at the counter and turned with such quick anger, I could tell she was ready for a good old-fashioned argument. "I mean," she said, coming toward the table and sitting down next to me, but glaring across the table, "Rita's face must be really hard for such a big guy like Rick to hurt his hand on."

"It wasn't like that at all," Mrs. Collins shot back. "Really, May! Rick was ashamed of himself. He's never done anything like that before. He was just hurt that Rita would break up with him. He told me he'd already bought her a ring and was planning to give it to her."

"He must be feeling real ashamed then," I said. I heard a quiver in my voice, both from anger and nervousness. "Just last week he beat on his little brother, Casey. Or did he kind'a fail to mention that?"

Mama's jaw dropped to hear May and me attacking Mrs. Collins, and there were questions in her eyes. I decided I needed to tell her, not only about Rick beating up on Casey, but about him telling Mrs. Collins about Lance and me. And I figured it might be time to tell her about what Margie had tried with me. I wouldn't have considered it, except that Margie seemed to be trying to defend Rick, where there was no defense. I wondered, too, just what it was between the two of them—her and Rick. Then I figured I already knew. Rick was probably one of her more interesting affairs, out of which had come a kind of rogue's friendship.

"If you ask me, Will Barnett," Mrs. Collins said, rising and wagging a finger at me, apparently as ready to do battle as May was, "you're just a little more than an innocent in all this. None of this would have come out the way it did if it wasn't for you and—"

"Shut up, Margie!" May said, also rising. "We've had just about enough of this. Even if Rick didn't like what he saw in our house, he could have kept his friggin' trap shut, if you ask me. But no! He decided to take things a little further by telling you. Isn't that right? And you! You thought it was a good opportunity to pluck a little young fruit!"

The secret was out now, and Mama looked from May to Margie and then at me. "What is she talking about, Will?"

Which 'she' Mama meant, I didn't know, but I was sick of the arguing, especially with Rita hurt and in bed. "Mrs. Collins is mistaken, Mama, that's all. Rita told me herself she was planning to break up with Rick. Maybe she found out things about him she just didn't care for."

I caught Margie's eye as I said this, and saw that she was a little relieved I'd steered Mama away from what May had just said, though she still looked angry.

She grabbed her purse from the table, turning to Mama. "I didn't mean to stir up any trouble, Arlene. Tell Trinket I'm waiting on her in the car."

* * *

With Trinket and Mrs. Collins suddenly gone, Mama and May and Lance and I just sat quietly for a moment at the kitchen table, each of us digesting what had just happened. Mama was still wearing the blue, terrycloth robe from the night before, and I could tell she hadn't got any more sleep than I had. May wasn't dressed yet, either, and was wearing a robe, as well, but underneath she had on a T-shirt. Lance and I were just wearing our Levi's and were both barefoot. It was kind of cold in the kitchen, because Mama hadn't turned on the furnace and usually didn't in mid-fall unless it was freezing.

The heat from the stove had all but dissipated, and we all cupped our hands around our coffee mugs.

Mama mashed out her cigarette, took a sip of coffee, and looked across the table at me and then at May. "Now, why don't you two tell me what's been going on, here." Her face was set, and I figured she already had a few ideas about things. She hadn't missed Lance's busted lip from a few weeks before, but when she'd asked him what happened, he just said it was an accident.

May and I exchanged glances, and I saw from the look in her eyes that she knew Mama wasn't going to put up with us sugar-coating anything. Both of us usually did try to soften things on Mama, because…well, she was Mama, and we didn't like to see her fret.

"Part of it has to do with me and Lance," I told Mama. "Rick figured out we were sleeping together." I eyed Mama, but she didn't seemed fazed by what I just said.

"Go on, Will," she said. "I've heard people talking, too. I don't like what you and Lance are doing, if you want to know."

"But—"

Mama just held up a hand. "Let me finish. I wouldn't like it ten years from now, I guess, so it couldn't be any worse, now." Then she looked at Lance, who lowered his eyes. "Lance, honey. I love you like a son, so please don't think I'm condemning you. Nor you, either, son," she said, turning back to me. "It's just something I was raised not to like. It's hard to change. Only I know that something's been going on because of that, something that got Lance hurt and now Rita. So let's get it on the table and deal with it."

Mama hadn't strung so many words together in a long time, at least since before Daddy died, and I was stunned. I figured she stayed home most of the time because she didn't want to face things in Hachita, much less in Animas and Cotton City, and just preferred staying where things were familiar, even if she was a little lonely.

I told her about Rick telling Mrs. Collins about me and Lance, and the day she tried to get in my pants. Mama's eyes flared, then she nodded, smiling kind of oddly. "I'm sorry she put you through that, Will.

But don't be too upset. She's a lonely woman. She's been a lot of boys' first experience with a woman. I'm glad you turned her down, though."

I was stunned, again, but kind of glad that what Mrs. Collins had tried with me wasn't going to make Mama hate her. May was struck dumb, though, and started laughing.

"Mama! Really! You don't sound the least bit surprised!"

Mama smiled. "Let's just forgive her that, May. And if you can't forgive her, just pity her."

Lance just looked at all of us with his jaw dropped and kind of smiled.

Then I told Mama why I'd agreed to pay Mr. Trujillo so much money for the harvest, after he'd tried to force me into paying twice that much, though I left out the part about the shotguns. I told her he thought he could get away with it because of the talk about me. Mama just nodded.

Then I told her about Rick's younger brother, Casey, and how Rick had beat him up for standing up to him about me and Lance.

"So that's why Margie said you had a little hand in all this, isn't it?" Mama asked. I opened my mouth to explain, but she just raised her hand again. "Well, she's wrong. Those Zumwalts have always been trouble for as long as I can remember. And I didn't like it that Rita was dating Rick, if you want to know. But just like I couldn't stop you, Will, from being who you are, I couldn't stop her, and I just didn't try. I grieved thinking she was getting serious enough to marry him. I've seen Leona Zumwalt wear sunglasses enough to know that her husband beats on her."

At this, I felt my stomach flip. "You mean they're all like that?"

Mama nodded. "Them and a few other families I could name, Will. Farming is a tough life and brings out people's frustrations, and some of the people that moved into this region brought their wife-beating ways with them."

During all this, May hadn't said much, and she still didn't, but I saw she was taking in as much as I was, maybe even realizing like me that Mama kept a lot of information to herself. But this morning, Mama was laying it out and asking us to do the same. And I realized that Mama thought of us more as adults that she could talk to than she did children she needed to protect. At least it felt like that to me.

May and I filled Mama in on other details about the way people had been talking, and I told her I thought things would just die down, now that Rick wouldn't be coming around.

"Maybe," she said. She got up and poured herself another cup of coffee and came back to the table and lit another cigarette. "But things is gonna change, Will. We've got this harvest over with. I think it's time we retired from farming and sold out. Your daddy's dead and gone, and he's the only one that ever wanted to keep this god-forsaken place. It killed him, and I see that you're about as worn out as you can be."

I was stunned and speechless, and so was May. Lance just looked at each of us, kind of bowing his head, but when tears glistened on his lower lashes, I asked him what was wrong. He shook his head. "I…" he looked up at Mama, then me, his face stricken. "I love this place, Will! I don't want it to be over!"

Mama looked surprised. She smiled at him. "It's all right, Lance, honey. First of all, we're not going to be moving out tomorrow. We'll be here at least until you graduate. We're just going to take a year off from farming and give us all a chance to rest."

Lance still didn't look too pleased, though he smiled back weakly at Mama. "It's the only real home I ever had, though!"

"But you'll always have a home with this family," Mama said, "no matter where that is." Her own eyes got a little wet. "It's just that, since Roy died, Goddard Hill has been making noises about buying us out. He wants the well and wants to return this place to pasture."

I thought it was a good idea, and I sure liked the idea of having the farm off my shoulders. "I hope he gives us a good price, Mama," I said, looking at her and then at Lance.

"Well, we're not going to give it away," she said.

* * *

It was almost seven-thirty when we all left the table. May rushed to shower, and Lance and I went out to the pickup to bring in his stuff from the night before. I'd decided to play hooky with him. He was quiet as we brought in his suitcase and the other stuff he'd brought back from his trip.

He was still quiet when we got into the bedroom.

"I didn't know you liked it here so much," I said.

He'd set his suitcase on the floor and was standing by the bed where he had laid the other packages, looking down at them. He spoke without looking at me. "I figured you and me would be leaving here, Will, one day. But..."

"What?"

He shrugged, then turned to look at me. He was smiling sadly. "It's the only place I've ever felt loved. It's hard to separate that from this room, and this house, and the barn and the fields."

I went over to him and hugged him from behind, and he put his hands on my forearms and held me tight. I felt him sob, then take a breath. "But your mother meant it, didn't she, about me always having a home with this family?"

I turned him around and looked into his beautiful violet eyes and the fear in them. We hugged, chest to chest, our skin warm. "She meant it, Lance. You bet. Always," I said. I didn't want to make light of his fear and sadness, or whatever it was, but I thought maybe it was something we would have to revisit later on.

So, after he smiled more broadly and looked more relieved, I smiled back. "Now, didn't you say something about a surprise for me last night?"

"Oh, yeah," he said, drawling on the last syllable. "Step back against the door and close your eyes."

I did as he said, leaning against the closed bedroom door with my eyes clamped shut. I heard the rustle of paper as he pulled things out of the packages. I couldn't imagine what it was.

"Okay. Open!"

I opened my eyes and blinked and found myself staring into a landscape of tall, dominating mountains, richly rendered in blues and hues of purple, against a clear turquoise sky, and in the foreground was a nude figure, facing away from the viewer, with both arms raised as if in greeting to the mountains. The light from our northwest windows didn't cause a glare, and I could study the fine details. It was a chalk pastel picture, I realized, having seen Lance work with the box of oil-based chalks he'd bought through the art class.

"Well?" he asked, looking at me over the painting.

"It's beautiful! But how did you get it so finished looking? You were only gone four days."

"I worked on it at night in the motel when everybody else was asleep. I got one look at the Sangre de Cristos, Will, and just knew I could represent them. And your body, I've got down in my mind's eye like a photograph."

"Well, I'm framing that," I said, "and it's going right here in our room, for anyone who comes in here to see."

# Ten
# Dick and Casey—Finally

We returned to school on Friday, and as soon as Lance and I parted, Casey and Dick found me and dragged me off behind the football stadium, both of them looking pleased with themselves, though Casey's face was still a mess of blue bruises and healing cuts. I didn't even want to think how his back must look full of scabbed-over slashes from the razor strap.

The weather had turned a little colder and I was wearing a shirt over my T-shirt, a Levi jacket, and a denim cap, with John Deere sewn in green above the bill. Dick was wearing a blue FFA corduroy jacket with the collar turned up, and Casey was wearing his windbreaker and beneath that a sweat shirt. A wind was whistling through the chain link fence, but we were all used to the cold and the wind.

"Where's Lance?" Dick asked, still looking pleased with himself.

I told him about the trip to northern New Mexico and how Lance was hot to be with the Barker twins and Mr. Drummond. "They've got lots of stuff they want to share with the others and lots of ideas they want to try." Which is about all I really understood about Lance's art, other than that he was great at it.

I saw something in Dick's face that I'd never seen before. He sure wasn't good looking, but when he looked pleased or was smiling like he was now, he was a whole lot better looking. I figured the ugliness came from his being unhappy, which his thin lips and rather sharp eyes didn't help.

"I kind'a wish he was here, though," Dick said. The three of us were facing each other. The sun was bright and the sky was clear. Off toward the school, I could hear the buzz of the other students who were still outdoors laughing and talking. But we were far enough away that you couldn't hear what they were saying, or really see them because of the bleachers in the stadium.

"I do, too," Casey said, looking at me, then smiling at Dick.

I figured that with both of them looking pleased and wishing Lance was with us, Casey's confession to Dick had gone well, but when they suddenly turned and kissed each other on the mouth, I just about burst out laughing, before I realized what they were doing—and why. It was a quick kind of kiss, though, and a moment later they were both looking at me, Casey with his eyebrows raised, and Dick with a grin on his face so big it looked like the crescent moon. I couldn't help but notice a tent in Dick's Levi's.

"That was for you," Dick said, kind of laughing, then looking embarrassed.

I still felt like laughing but knew I better not. "For me? You're trying to tell me something, guys?" I was sure I had already guessed, but I wanted to play dumb.

"Aw, geez, Dick Tracy, what gave you your first clue?" Casey said. He threw his arm around Dick's shoulders and reached over as bold as you please and cupped Dick's crotch.

"You told him, didn't you?" I asked Casey.

"Everything," Dick said. "About you and Lance, 'bout Casey being his brothers' little plaything, which makes me mad enough to spit!"

It was like walking into an episode of The Twilight Zone for a minute, until everything sank in. Not only had Dick obviously not freaked out, like I was afraid he would, but he and Casey had already carried it to the next step.

"And have you guys...?" I raised my eyebrows and looked at them.

Casey was grinning, looking pitiful because of the bruises and happy at the same time. "Just about every place we could think of," he said.

"Oh, man!" Dick added. "Don't know if you know or not, Will, but I never got any, like I was always saying."

I knew he meant sex with girls, though I never believed him to begin with, because he had always seemed so interested in me and then Lance, even if he tried to cover over it by being hateful to us.

"And are you guys, like, boyfriends, now?"

They both just laughed. They both looked embarrassed. They glanced at each other, then back at me.

"I guess so," Dick said, "if you gotta call it that. Yeah." Then he looked at Casey as if for approval. "Maybe so."

Casey smiled a little more wisely at me and nodded. "Sure we are."

They had a long way to go, I figured, before they'd be feeling as easy with it as me and Lance.

When the bell rang, all three of us jumped, though we still had about fifteen minutes. I didn't know what else to say, so I stuck out my hand and shook theirs, finding my tongue stuck and unable to congratulate them, though I thought I should say something. "That's cool, guys. You wanna tell Lance yourselves?"

"I do," Dick said. "I owe him a big apology, don't you think? Now that...I...now that we're kind of brothers, or whatever you call it."

* * *

Brothers. I think I like that. Gay brothers. I think I'll remember it. I've just written down my impressions from yesterday morning when Dick and Casey talked to me out back of the school. I can't help but think how different it would have been if the four of us had been friends and "out" to each other longer. We were the only ones I knew of—gay, that is. Though now that Dick's been initiated, if you want to call it that, and he and Casey are exploring each other, I'm thinking it's more like what Lance said about the other men he did it with back in New Orleans. I'll get to that in a minute, though. I want to write down about last night.

It was our last football game of the season and my last game forever. We played Cobre, a town from up near Silver City. We waxed them on our home field, and then everybody went to the homecoming dance, except for me and Lance and Casey and Dick. Dick had his mother's Chevy and seemed really hot for the four of us to take off by ourselves. I kind of wish Lance and I hadn't gone because of what happened; in another way, though, most of it was kind of neat—that gay brothers thing.

So Dick and Casey sat in the front and Lance and I sat in the back. Dick called it a double date, though he sounded embarrassed and kept laughing kind of nervously. It's true, though. We didn't have our own ideas about what you would call it, except calling it a date. So that's what it was, and I guess it embarrassed Dick because of that.

The first mistake we made was drinking beer. Like I've said, before, Daddy didn't believe in drinking and I never touch the stuff. Even back before Lance, when I was hanging out with Dick and a few of the guys from the football team, and we would run around in Animas and Cotton City, someone would always get beer and, after I'd tasted it a couple of times, I was through with it. I never could get past a few sips. But last night, as soon as Lance and I got in the back seat, Dick announced he had some beer and wanted us to go somewhere and drink it. Then he took off out of the school parking lot and we headed out of Animas, straight south down Highway 338. It was dark out, but you could see the Animas Mountains close to the highway on the east and the Peloncillo Mountains a little farther off to the west—big, hulking masses on either side of the highway.

Pretty soon, Casey started messing with the six pack of beer, and I heard the can opener sink into the top with a sploosh! Sploosh!, then he handed it foaming back to me. At least it was cold, so I figured I could gag it down. Then he opened another can and he handed it over the seat to Lance. We were already sitting close together behind the driver's side. I had my right arm around him, and we glanced at each other when we had our beers.

"You ever drink beer?" I asked him, quietly, and I could see him nod, though his head was kind of just a silhouette, but his beer can glinted in what little light there was, and even the foam oozing out of the top of our cans was lit like spider webs in moonlight.

I started in drinking mine fast, because I hated the taste, and I just wanted to get it over with. As it was, I only got about a quarter of it down, before I decided I'd sip on the rest. Something about Lance I didn't know was he could handle it pretty well. Though, like me, he took a couple of chugs and then sipped it. But up in front, Casey and Dick drank like their fathers must do at the bars on a Saturday night. They were through with their first beers in no time and just started in on the second ones.

So far, we hadn't done much talking. Casey wasn't sitting too close to Dick, though he had his left arm over the seat back and was kind of playing his fingers through Dick's hair. He was kind of turned in the seat, too, and I could tell he was looking back at us.

You can go almost any direction out of Animas and, in a little while, be isolated, especially as late at night as it was, so when Dick came to a dirt road heading off toward the west, he turned off and drove about a mile then pulled to a stop. As soon as the engine died and he killed the lights, the silence of the desert, and the dark light of the sky, the silhouette of the mountains—all just grabbed my attention. It never fails to inspire my own silence, the way this country dominates and dwarfs you.

And I guess it inspired the same quiet in everybody, because nobody spoke for a while. All you could hear was us taking drinks in the dark.

Then Dick half turned in the seat and his profile was lit by the night, a shiny cheek, the glint of his eye. He was looking at Lance, and I saw him grin, because his teeth showed ever so slightly. "I never meant for you to get hurt," he said.

Lance and I both knew what Dick was talking about.

"Well, I didn't get hurt," Lance said. He squeezed my leg. "So it's all right." The way he said it, the last word was strong with his southern drawl, and in the dark, in the car, his deep, oily voice sent a little shiver up my back.

"He could'a been, though," I said and took a sip of beer. It also made me shiver, it tasted so nasty.

Dick was still leaning over the seat, his beer can glinting light. He took a gulp, burped, and stuck out his hand. "Shake though?" he said to Lance. "I swear, little buddy, all of us were assholes, and I was the worst. Only game we lost was that night, and Will's right, I was stupid." Dick's speech was kind of slurred, with a drunk accent.

His hand lingered over the seat, and Lance finally shook it. "It's all right," Lance said, again.

I didn't know what was going through Lance's mind, though he seemed a little hesitant to friendly up to Dick. But it was a better apology than Casey had offered that Monday morning after the incident.

"We're buddies, though, right?" Dick said. By now, Casey had turned in the seat and was looking back at us, too. For some reason, the whole thing seemed kind of awkward. The four of us in the middle of nowhere.

The night was chilly, so our windows were up, and the smell of the beer permeated the air, and with both Dick and Casey leaning over the seat and talking to us, their beer breath smelled strong. I decided to get mine over with and chugged it. When I came up for air, I felt a little light headed and a little sick to my stomach, as a bubble of air worked its way up my windpipe.

When I did belch, everybody laughed, which kind of broke the awkwardness. Lance chugged his, too, and when Dick and Casey chugged theirs, I thought we were through with the beer, but I heard the sound of another can being opened and kind of sighed to myself, realizing they had more than a six pack.

So we sat there and finished off the second six pack, making two for me and two for Lance, and four apiece for Dick and Casey. Conversation came easily, if not too clearly as Dick went on about how he'd always felt something for guys, and how he knew it was wrong, and it made him sick, and when he first thought I was queer (his word), it scared him, but he just couldn't get it out of his head.

"I gotta tell you, Will," he said, his speech slurred more than ever, and a kind of sob escaping from him, "I jacked off to you ever since we were freshmen, and you never gave me the ti…time of, hic, day."

I didn't say anything, except belch.

"And then when you got Lance at your house, I seen how…" he trailed off, rubbing his face.

Suddenly, he kind of plowed into Casey, wrapping his arms around him and kissing him. From the way they looked, two half-lit silhouettes in the dark, with the light of the night sky back lighting them—obviously both guys—it kind of turned me on. It was neat. An image I'd never seen, since I never saw Lance and me kiss. It brought home exactly what the four of us were, and why we had to drive all the way out here to be together.

So I turned and pulled Lance to me just then, feeling a little hot, and he came at me with the same urgency, and there for a few minutes, as we were kissing and getting each other's faces wet, and Casey and Dick were doing the same thing, all I could hear was the sound of us four guys going at each other. It was just like guys and girls did when they went parking, I supposed—something I'd never done. Something that, until now, I never realized I'd missed. Same for Dick and Casey, I guess.

Then Dick let out a whoop, and I could hear the joy in his voice. Oddly, his expression of that joy through his hollering meant something to me, as if he'd spoken words, about the loneliness that all four of us must have felt all our lives. It also said we didn't have to feel lonely, anymore.

Lance and I came up for air. I had a stiff-on, and so did he. We were holding the bulges in the other's pants. Then Dick and Casey came up for air, and they hung over the seat, again, kind of laughing, running their hands over each other's shoulders.

"You guys doing all right?" Dick asked.

I kind of wished he would pay more attention to Casey and not me and Lance. I was hurting I was so stiff, and this was the first time that Lance and I couldn't make love—not in front of them. So I had to endure the pain of wanting him.

"I need to take a leak," Casey said, and as he was opening his door, I noticed that the windows were all steamed up from the heat we had been generating there in the car. Just that fact of how physical we had all been spoke to me as well.

A moment later, all of us stepped out. Lance followed me out on my side and together we moved a little ways off and turned our backs on Casey and Dick. We'd never just peed together, either, but we whipped out our little buddies standing side by side, and I was feeling a little woozy, so I put my arm around Lance for support, and he did the same; then we both let go at the same time, sending arcs of beer water shining in the starlight onto the ground. When I was finished, with my arm still around Lance, I looked up.

It never failed to thrill me at the heavens out here in the desert so far from any real lights. The sky was rivers of stars, from horizon to horizon, so densely full, only gaps of blackness showed through like clear patches of sky on a cloudy day. It was light enough that I could see the clumps of grease wood and mesquite on the valley floor around us, and make out large boulders sitting on the sides of the Animas Mountains to the east. In the west, the Peloncillos were darker, more massive, and less distinct. But it was light enough by the starlight alone that I could see back down the dirt road.

Then Lance turned me to him and pulled me down to meet his lips, as he wrapped his arms around me and kissed me on the mouth, whispering, "I love you so much, Will, it hurts! Do you know that?"

"Me too, baby. I want us to make love, but—"

"Not here," he finished for me. "It wouldn't be right."

"It wouldn't," I agreed.

So when we went back to the car, I was surprised to see that Casey and Dick were now making out leaning up against the hood of the car. Casey's naked butt was shining in the light, and I saw that Dick had his pants down around his ankles and they were kind of masturbating each other.

I took Lance's hand and pulled him down the road a little ways. I couldn't stand it anymore, so even though it was cold, we moved off into a stand of boulders. In a few moments, we were both naked and did our sixty-nine thing out of sight of Dick and Casey.

Just as we were about to finish, I looked up. I saw that Casey and Dick had followed us and, apparently, had been watching. That's when I wished we hadn't come, because it made me feel like this was wrong, being watched, and I didn't like it, so I pulled Lance up, and when he noticed them, he scrambled into his clothes.

Dressed, we didn't say anything, but went back to the car. Dick and Casey followed.

"Man, that was hot!" Dick said, as they came up to us.

"It wasn't for you!" I snapped.

"But why not?" he asked, his voice still slurred. "We're all queer, here!"

I didn't know what to say. Lance had gone kind of silent, but he squeezed my hand. "It's all right, Angel," he said. Then to Dick: "It's okay, man."

"My brothers used to watch each other do me," Casey said, quietly. "It's just the way they did it. One of them would get the idea it was time for a little fun with baby brother—"

"Don't, man!" Dick said. "That makes it sound sick. I don't like that!"

So then we all got silent, each feeling a kind of shame, I guess, though mine was not so much shame as it was an embarrassed anger.

What I meant about Dick and Casey being more like the guys back in New Orleans is that there wasn't the love between Lance and those guys he went with on the streets. He hustled them for a place to stay and for food. But between Lance and me it was love. I'm not so sure if it's that between Casey and Dick, though, because last night, they both seemed to be in it for the sex. Why else would they enjoy watching me and Lance and not just make love together as Lance and I did?

When we were all back in the car, each of us probably having finished, I guess, in our own way, there didn't seem to be much interest in staying out there. Without asking, Dick started the engine, made a three-point turn, and headed back down the road.

When we pulled into the school parking lot, I was surprised that the homecoming dance was apparently still going on. Here and there in the parking lot, groups of guys and girls were screaming and laughing and having a good time. It was the first time, ever, since Lance and I have been together, that I felt the enormity of the difference between being gay and not being gay. What Lance and I have, and what Dick and Casey want, has to be hidden and furtive, while here at the school, the guy-girl dates can be done openly, even if some of them are just in it for the sex, too.

Of course, I'm realizing this as I write in this journal. All that didn't hit me when it was happening.

I've read this over, and I don't mean to sound so judgmental and maybe even superior to Dick. I understand the pent-up frustration that finally having sex can release, and which makes you want to keep doing it till you're raw and sore. It was like that for me with Lance, and maybe it was the same for him, because we sure went at it a lot at first, only now diminishing to once and sometimes twice a night.

It's just now Saturday morning. With the harvest finished and nothing to do to prepare the fields, since Mama said we're going to sell out, I woke up lazily and didn't worry about getting out of bed. I still woke up at five, and after Lance woke up, we just lay there kissing and staring into each other's eyes and talking about last night with Dick and Casey.

He laughed about it this morning—us putting on the show for them. Of course we didn't know they were watching us, and when we realized it, we both deflated fast.

"I hope you didn't hurt Dick's feelings," Lance said. "You kind of sounded angry at him."

"I was, Lance. Geez. It made it kind of…"

"Dirty?" he asked.

"Well…no…not dirty because with you, it's always been so beautiful. But it's also always been private."

"Still," he said. "I think I need to talk things out with Dick. Let him know he's got the rest of his life to get used to it."

I knew what Lance was saying, because it kind of echoed what I had been thinking as he and I lay there, this morning. "He's just into the sex part, right now. Is that what you mean?"

"Kind of, Angel. I remember when you and I first knew we were going to make love. You wouldn't do it in the pickup. You wouldn't do it in the barn." He laughed, his languid laughter deep-throated, which never fails to turn me on and make me just want to hug him to me. "You just had to be in bed." I had my right arm under Lance's neck, and he turned his head so that his breath tickled my cheek. "Right?" he asked.

I rolled him to me, felt his thighs against my own, felt his warmth, felt us both throbbing down there. "Right," I said, beginning to tongue his lips. "And I'm glad we waited like that. But you're right. I know what Dick is going through, and we both need to let him know what he did last night was all right. I was kind of angry. But not now."

"Then you want to go parking with them again?" This time Lance's voice went up in a question, and there was mocking in it, a challenge.

"No. This time I think you and me ought'a watch them. Since you're the experienced one, you can teach them things they may not have thought of. Like you've been teaching me."

"They'll have to discover it for themselves," Lance said, tonguing me back, and pressing himself against me.

We disappeared under the covers, pulling the blanket up over our heads, and did a little steaming up of our own. This time the smells permeating the air were of our familiar body scents, the particularly sweet mustiness of our sex, the rest of the day promising nothing but being with each other in our new-found freedom from the demands of the farm.

# *Eleven*
# *Dirty Talk*

Mama was right. I never knew how tired and used up I was until it was coming up on Christmas and I realized I didn't have to get up early before school to get the disk and plow ready, and sleeping in until six in the morning was a luxury.

In fact, I was eager to wrap up my classes with unaccustomed enjoyment. Though my grades had never slipped, as they had my freshman year, I was suddenly on fire and spent hours in the evenings doing my homework with the same kind of heat Lance poured into his painting.

And with football season over, Casey, Dick, Lance, and I did go out together, again and again. We were truly becoming the gay brothers Dick had talked about. But we didn't have any more of those late-night make-out sessions in front of each other. I chalk it up to the fact that both Dick and Casey had been a lot more drunk than Lance and I were that night, and they probably wouldn't have thought to watch us, otherwise. I realized that was one of the things Daddy always had against drinking. People were more apt to do things when they're drunk that they would never do sober.

But Lance forced all four of us into what was at first embarrassing talks about being gay and having sex. He did it because he wanted Casey and Dick to think about things; but he also did it because he knew a few little secrets that he'd shown me, and he wanted them to enjoy their time together. So as I had playfully suggested that morning after we had all gone out parking, Lance did instruct them, amazed that even though Casey had been abused by his brothers, but especially Rick, they had more or less just pawed at him, like adolescent boys might paw at their girlfriends, and hadn't really done more than penetrate him. "It hurt like hell," Casey admitted, "except a few times."

So Lance shared our secret of glycerin and rosewater with them, and one day after that, we were talking about it during lunch, and Dick and Casey both looked goofy-happy, from what must have been a night of real love-making, which made us all laugh, until we realized that some of our graphic talk was getting out of hand because, when Stephen Zumwalt passed by our table with a nasty look, Casey almost went white with fear.

"Do you think he heard? Do you? Do you know what they'd do to me at home if they thought—"

So we all tried to cool it after that. Only seeing how uncomfortable Casey looked, I can't help but think that he would have it a lot harder than me or even Lance if Rick ever really knew his baby brother was gay. So I hope nothing ever comes of what Stephen might have heard.

# Twelve
# Transitions

Just a couple of days before Christmas, May announced that she was moving out by the end of the month. Mama didn't seem to be distressed or anything. And I knew why. We would all be moving out when Lance graduated at the end of next year, so knowing that May was going to have a place before then was really more of a comfort than something to worry over or be sad about.

"Are you moving in with Kelsey Snow?" I asked May when we were alone. It was an odd sort of day, kind of cloudy but warm for December. May and I were out at the barn. She was getting a look at where she and I had spent so much time with Daddy. In fact, she was walking all over that morning. I think she was trying to burn the place into her memory. Of any of the girls, May came closer than her sisters to really loving this place, and much of her own sweat had gone into making it work.

She didn't answer my question right away about where she was moving. Instead, she ran her hand along one of the tractor tires as we passed by the old International Harvester. "Would you mind too much, Will, if I took Daddy's tools? You're not going to need them, are you?"

For a moment my stomach wrenched with sadness. I hadn't thought of the personal things like Daddy's tools that would be scattered and lost forever, once we sold the farm. "Of course not. I'm not going to need them when I go to college. And I'm sure Mama wouldn't mind."

"Thanks," she said. "I'm moving in with Kelsey, if you must know."

I was a little hurt with the way she put it. "Come on, May, you don't have to be so secretive with me, do you? You don't think I know what it is between you and Kelsey?"

She stopped in her tracks, and turned to face me fully. Her look reminded me of the hot-tempered sister, the freckle-faced tomboy, the same sister who had gone with me over to Playas to pick up Lance the night he told his parents he was leaving. Her eyes flared, and then she kind of smiled sadly. "It's not you, Will. It's not me, either. Kelsey is a basket case when it comes to people finding out, and I promised her I wouldn't tell anyone. She's been freaked to see the way people treated you and Lance."

"Well, then you guys should pack up and leave Hachita. What's here that you just have to stay?"

At this, May smiled more like she wasn't angry or sad. "The Snow ranch. Will it's absolutely beautiful. Half of it's in New Mexico, and the other half is in Arizona. She's the only child, and she's going to inherit it. Her parents are old, and even if Kelsey has to work to help pay the taxes, she's going to hang onto it. Who knows, one of these days, we might turn it into a resort. It's got pine forests and a lake and these old Indian ruins. There's nobody around for miles."

I was surprised. May had never said boo about Kelsey's family, and I had never asked. But I respected Kelsey's fear, I guess. I didn't know how May was going to handle having to be so secretive—not that she was reckless like me, but she was pretty independent and opinionated. I didn't think Kelsey would get away for long telling her she couldn't do this or that. My mouth watered, however, at the thought of her one day living on all that land. Especially land like the Snow ranch covered. The stunning thing about this southwestern part of New Mexico is its hidden treasures. People pass through here, through the desert part, and keep right on driving, probably thinking it's all harsh desert. People who have lived here all their lives just smile and keep their secrets.

* * *

Even though Daddy hadn't even been dead six months and we all missed him, with Lance in our lives, Christmas this year was one of the most joyous I ever remember. Julianne and Marsha called that morning and spoke to all of us, saying how they wished they could be there, since it was the first Christmas without Daddy, but they just couldn't. I didn't expect them to come. They never did. It was Lance's and my first Christmas together, and I had gone all out to make it special for him. But so had the girls and Mama. Mama took money out of savings and bought him a bunch of clothes. May and the girls had bought him cologne and socks and even some oil paints and canvases, and I had pitched in with other art supplies. But the most important for him was I had gone over to Deming one day while he was finishing up a painting he'd been working on for his art class. I bought us wedding bands. I debated with myself about presenting them to him along with the rest of the gifts, but I decided it was going to be special, if not completely secret, so I waited until after we'd all opened gifts before I sprung them on him.

Lance had done portraits of the girls and Mama, and me, and everybody got similarly wrapped packages from him. I felt tears welling up in my eyes at his embarrassment when his presents just kept piling up and he seemed afraid that we wouldn't like what he'd done for us. But that changed as soon as Mama opened her present from Lance. He had painted her from memory. No one knew he was doing portraits of the family, and yet, what he captured on canvas was remarkable, since he had painted them from memory, just as he had painted one of me when he was on his trip to northern New Mexico. Anyway, Mama burst into tears when she saw herself, so delighted she started crying and laughing, and asking us, "do I really look as good as this?" We all told her she did, didn't she know that? And yet, Lance had also captured her older age, without flinching from the wrinkles, but he had also captured Mama's inner self, so that her eyes crinkled not only with age as she looked out from the canvas, but with the kind of compassion and love Lance felt coming from her. He did the same with each of the girls. He captured Rita's seeming sense of style and the pride she took in her appearance. He revealed Trinket's playfulness and her intelligence. Trinket wanted to be a veterinarian or a doctor, and Lance had painted her reading a book, her eyes gazing intently at what she was reading, her mouth turned up in a young girl's smile. May was looking out from her portrait, freckles and all, but had never looked so handsome and competent.

I was surprised that Lance had given me a look that I felt was only inside me and not something the world sees. He made me look boyish and tough, but also revealed how I really saw myself. I can't describe it. I almost looked too soft, I guess, or as I used to think of Uncle Sean as pretty. I can feel heat rise to my face as I write this. I'm not trying to be vain. But inside, I do feel pretty. I was pleased that Lance brought it out in my face, much better than photos of me ever turned out.

So up onto the bookshelf next to the TV went all five paintings, and for a moment I felt sad that there wasn't one of Lance up there with the rest of us. But he was grinning from ear-to-ear, pleased that everyone liked his gifts.

Then, when we had picked up all the paper and ribbons and gifts, I took Lance to our room and sat him down on the bed, making him close his eyes. I sat down next to him with our rings in my hand. I took his right hand in mine, still with his eyes closed, though I could see him trying to see through his lashes, and kind of grinning. Then I placed my ring in his palm.

"Open your eyes," I said, getting a kick out of watching the expression of confusion, then understanding, light his face as he saw the ring.

"But I didn't get you one, Will! I didn't know you were—"

I kissed him on the mouth to shut him up and opened my palm for him to see. "This is your ring. That's mine," I said, indicating the one in his hand.

So, we went through a little wedding ceremony, right then, placing the rings on each other's ring finger of the right hand, laughing hysterically, when Lance said, in his best southern drawl, "I now pronounce us Mr. and Mr. Barfett!"

"Or Sur-Barn," I said.

"Or Nett-fett," he said, without missing a beat.

Then we collapsed on the bed, laughing. But in a moment he sat up, his face serious, looking me in the eyes with his own. They were a beautiful, untroubled violet. He took my hands in his and we entwined our fingers. "Whatever we call ourselves from now on doesn't matter. Just that we're two guys who love each other."

He looked embarrassed and thoughtful, and I felt the same. It wasn't a light moment for us. We had always made love desperately, many times with tears, and we had given each other bruised lips with the intensity with which we smashed them together, as if any minute we might be torn apart. Maybe it was the same with other people who loved each other. But I remember, even now, how Uncle Sean talked about his intense, though short, love with Theodore Seabrook, and how they were crazy for each other, and when they were apart, almost insane. That's how I felt about Lance, and I know that's how he felt about me.

Nothing would ever change that. I could see us as eighty-year-old men and breaking each other's fragile bones because we just couldn't help it as we clung tightly to each other.

* * *

Uncle Sean showed up the day after Christmas, the way he had done so many years before. It was almost like that first time, too, because when I went into the kitchen for breakfast, having slept in till almost seven, there he was talking to Mama and drinking coffee, his blond hair even more ragged than it was the first time I saw him, and when he turned in his chair and pierced my heart with those beautiful pale-blue eyes and smiled at me with those soft pink lips, I felt a sob start way down in my guts and tears spring to my eyes.

"Uncle Sean!"

"Hey, Will! How's it going?" he said, rising as I came up to him.

In an instant, we were hugging, hard arms around each other's backs, slapping each other's shoulders. Then we pulled away and grinned at each other. Damn, but he looked even better than before.

And I told him so. He appraised me and seemed speechless, then exclaimed, "you're all grown up!" as if he were surprised.

I caught Mama's face a second after we pulled apart, and though she was smiling, she was watching us with something going on behind her eyes. It was just a split-second kind of thing, and in a moment I was at the counter, pouring my coffee, feeling kind of embarrassed to be only in my Levi's and barefoot. And one other thing. I was still getting used to wearing my wedding band in front of the family, and even though nobody had said anything about it, I could tell that the girls were a little curious. I didn't know what Mama was feeling about it; she had chosen not to say. So, when I sat down across the corner of the table from Uncle Sean, I tried not to act nervous. But he noticed the ring and raised his eyebrows.

Mama had turned back to the counter and was dishing up some eggs and bacon for me and Uncle Sean.

He smiled at me, and I told him softly, "we put them on, yesterday. I've never forgotten those guys we saw at the movies in Deming, remember?"

"No, Will. I haven't forgotten, either. Not them, not the movie, not anything." The way he said it, I knew he was talking about the time we kissed in the car.

"Me neither," I said. Then it struck me. "What...what brings you here?"

By this time Mama had set our plates in front of us and had retreated to her end of the table with her coffee and cigarettes.

Uncle Sean glanced at his sister, then back at me. "As I was telling Arlene, Will, I just graduated with my business degree, and I'm heading out to Austin, Texas. I got a job with a new electronics company. It's a ground floor kind of thing."

I didn't know what to say. I was glad to see him, but a little disturbed about his leaving California. I had spent many nights dreaming about me and Lance moving out to San Francisco. I had read about Berkeley, had seen the anti-war protests on TV, had seen the hippies — all that. It was such a different kind of life, it had seemed unreal to me, but had also seemed like a kind of paradise for me and Lance. Uncle Sean had often told me about areas, there, where gay men congregated, where he had met his last boyfriend. So, with his announcement that he was moving to Texas, I began to wonder about a lot of things. Things I couldn't talk about in front of Mama.

My thoughts were interrupted, however, when Lance came into the kitchen. Like me, he was shirtless and barefoot. He kind of stopped dead in his tracks when he saw Uncle Sean, though I don't think he knew for sure if it was Uncle Sean. Clear as a glint of sunlight on a windshield, his wedding band caught the light pouring into the kitchen from the east window.

I got up quickly and stood by him. "Uncle Sean, this is Lance," I said, putting my arm across his shoulders and grinning, despite how Mama might be taking it. Though I figured she would do all right.

Uncle Sean got up and he and Lance shook hands, both of them smiling at the other, though Lance looked kind of shy. I was proud of him and was glad I could show him off to Uncle Sean. I'd described Lance a million different ways to Uncle Sean over the phone, as I had described Uncle Sean to Lance, and here they were meeting for the first time.

I loved them both so much, I was about to cry with joy. And I was able to settle something in my mind, just then, something I hadn't really asked myself, consciously. I knew the answer to that unasked question, however, as soon as it came to my mind.

Even though Uncle Sean was more beautiful than ever and all those old feelings for him came rushing back the moment I saw him at the table, the answer is I would choose Lance. I didn't think I should share this little conclusion with Uncle Sean or Lance, however.

My mind was filling with so many thoughts about Uncle Sean—why he chose to go to Texas, what happened to his last boyfriend, what would Lance and I do, now that we didn't have a place to head to if we chose to go to California—too many thoughts to concentrate on. So when the girls started drifting into the kitchen one-by-one and showing the same joy I felt at seeing Uncle Sean, all of us were carried away into the moment of greeting, of asking questions all at once, laughing, eating, and generally celebrating.

And then, just as he had done so many years ago, as well, Uncle Sean said he had to get some sleep, because he had driven all night and wondered where he could crash for awhile. So Lance and I took him into our bedroom and quickly changed the sheets and got him settled in.

But he sat on the bed, acting like he wasn't ready for us to leave, so I shut the door. I'd forgotten about the painting that Lance had done for me up in northern New Mexico. I had made a frame for it and, as I shut the door, Uncle Sean saw it.

"Nice," he said. "Who did it?"

I told him Lance had.

"You said he was an artist, Will, but you never indicated just how good he is. I know men back in San Francisco who would kill for something like that." Then he got up and came up to Lance, putting a hand on his shoulder, still looking at the painting from close up. "You could sell something like that, Lance, for quite a bit of cash."

Lance was pleased, but embarrassed, though he seemed to like the attention Uncle Sean was paying him. He glanced at me, smiling.

I looked at both of them standing close together and my heart thumped. If I took myself out of the picture and it was just the two of them, I could imagine them falling in love. They looked really good together. I projected myself into a scene where they did fall for each other, and were telling me that they were sorry, but...

"...why I'm here," Uncle Sean said.

He had apparently said something more, and I just caught the tail end.

"Why? I thought you just stopped by since it was on your way."

He returned to the bed, and pulled off his shoes, leaving Lance and me standing by the painting.

"I'm bushed, Will. I am on my way to Austin, but I was hoping, if you and Arlene don't mind, that I could stay until the first of the year. I need you, again, I'm afraid."

"Need me, Uncle Sean?"

He passed his hand over his eyes, then looked up at us, and I could see pain in his face. "To talk the way you and I used to," he said, pulling off his shirt, then slipping out of his pants. He slid between the sheets.

In a moment, he shut his eyes, turned into a fetal position, and seemed to lose consciousness.

Lance pulled the sheet and blanket up around his shoulders and, without a word, we slipped quietly out of the room.

# Thirteen
# Things Lost

It broke my heart to see Uncle Sean so unhappy. Not that he wore it on his sleeve or anything. He wasn't like that. Whenever we talked on the telephone all those years after he left here and he was going to school, I asked him about his boyfriends. At first it was this one guy, who Uncle Sean said wasn't nearly as pretty as his Theodore Seabrook, who got murdered by "friendly fire" in Vietnam, and which sent Uncle Sean out of the service and into that hospital in San Antonio. Then it was another boyfriend, who Uncle Sean said was a "knockout," only I don't think Uncle Sean ever fell in love with him. And finally, it was this last guy, who Uncle Sean sounded like he loved, telling me, "I think he's the one, Will." Which was the last I knew until Uncle Sean got here the day after Christmas.

But when Lance and I put him up in our room that first morning so he could sleep, Uncle Sean had said he needed me to talk to him like we used to. So the first chance I got, I asked him if he'd like to see the farm.

That was just a signal that if he wanted to talk we could be alone. I was expecting him and me to spend a couple of hours alone together. I was sure Lance would understand. So I was surprised when Uncle Sean asked Lance to come along. When all three of us were a little ways from the house, Uncle Sean said, "I hope you don't mind, Will, but I wanted Lance to come with us."

I didn't mind and said so, but Lance seemed a little uneasy about it and said he didn't want to intrude.

But Uncle Sean insisted. "It's important to me, Lance. I don't have much time to stay, and you and Will are part of each other. I want to feel the two of you together. Will and I always talked about getting him a boyfriend, and Will says you're that guy."

I was embarrassed, but Uncle Sean's words made Lance smile—and that made me feel warm.

Anyway, it turned out that Uncle Sean was running away from San Francisco by taking that job in Austin. He was running away from the way his last boyfriend had hurt him.

"He didn't come home one night," Uncle Sean said. Lance and I and Uncle Sean were out in the barren fields where the corn crop had been. It was a cold, blustery afternoon and we all had on heavy jackets. Uncle Sean's longish blond hair whipped around his face as we walked and he had this habit of running his fingers through it, to get it away from his face. He'd lost some of the weight but not the muscle he'd had when he was here in 1969, fresh out of the army, and even his hands were thinner, though just as pretty. He looked honest to gosh more like an intellectual now than he did a soldier. Those years had made a difference in that way. His face was bonier, too, but he had such good looks, all the angles of his face made him look even prettier, his soft pink lips even more pronounced. Lance was walking on the other side of Uncle Sean, and like him, Lance's hair was longish. The last five months had made a difference in Lance's appearance, too. His hair was a burnished kind of sandy brown, and caught the gusts of wind, sometimes obscuring his violet eyes, sometimes lifting away from his face and revealing his own beauty. He had put on more weight since he had been here and the almost too bony features of his face were gone. He was deeply tanned from all our work outdoors and, compared to Uncle Sean, and even compared to what Lance had looked like when I first met him, he looked tougher, more confident. Yet his face revealed his own ache at Uncle Sean's sadness.

"And when he did get home, Will," Uncle Sean continued, about his last boyfriend, "he wouldn't tell me where he had been, though I saw he had hickies on his neck—big, deep, blood-red marks, like whoever he had been with had devoured him."

My stomach clenched at the thought of having Lance do that to me. I guess like Mrs. Collins cheated on her husband, Uncle Sean's boyfriend had cheated on him.

"Is that when you took off?" I asked, looking at Uncle Sean, but also past him to Lance and seeing Lance's concern, too, even though he hardly knew Uncle Sean.

I was on Uncle Sean's left, and he turned to look at me. It was either the cold wind causing his eyes to tear up or he was moist-eyed remembering, but he shook his head, his piercing blue eyes holding mine. "I hadn't graduated yet, Will. So I had to stay. I tried to forget what Dean had done. I tried not to think about it or talk to him about it, but I couldn't stop myself from asking. That's when he told me how dumb I was. Didn't I know that our 'marriage' was a cheap fake of a thing? What was I trying to do, he asked, be like straight people? He said men are naturally promiscuous and want to spread their sperm as far as they can and it was a social game to be monogamous."

That was a lot for me to take in, especially the promiscuous thing. It made me sad to think that his boyfriend thought he couldn't be married because they were just two men. "Is that how it is out there in San Francisco, then, Uncle Sean? Do all the men think like that?"

He took a deep breath, ran his fingers through his hair. "Probably not, Will," he said, looking at me and taking in Lance then kind of staring off toward the north, which is the direction we were headed. "But that's all I found. It's just that there are gay night clubs and bath houses, and San Francisco is full of gay men. Having sex with as many partners as you can is the thing to do."

I couldn't imagine. The way it took Casey and Dick so long to get together, and the way people hated the thought of Lance and me, ready to castrate Lance, ready to beat us both up, it was like being from a different planet. In a way, I could see Dick Lamb heading straight for San Francisco and loving it. Maybe even Casey.

"But that's not what you want, is it?" I asked.

He shook his head, still staring toward the horizon. "No. I want my Teddy, Will. And I can't have him."

I felt tears sting my eyes. "Or someone as mad about you as you are him." I also felt guilty, glancing at Lance, because I thought that's what he and I had, now.

When the sun began its quick descent toward the west and was just sinking behind the Peloncillo Mountains, the wind sort of died down and we all headed back to the house. It was almost a quarter of a mile away, and by the time we got there, it was coming on dusk, and there in the driveway was Mrs. Collins' Caddie.

"Hey, Uncle Sean," I said, trying out a lighter sounding voice, hoping to make a joke. "Margie Collins is here. She's always had the hots for you. Won't that help a little?"

He groaned and so did Lance. "Maybe you're right, Will. Maybe she's just what I need!" Then Uncle Sean kind of laughed, but it sounded forced.

* * *

May moved out a few days after Uncle Sean got here, and I helped her pack her stuff. She didn't have nearly as many clothes and things like that as Rita had, and everything she was taking with her fit into the back of my pickup. We didn't forget Daddy's tools, and a few other things from around the house. Still it wasn't much. It was kind of sad I told her after she had said good-bye to the other girls and Uncle Sean…and Mama. That's when May kind of got misty-eyed, when she hugged Mama good-bye. "I'll call you every day, Mama. And if Will needs any help you let me know, 'cause he sure won't call and ask."

Mama was crying. But everybody expected it. She was smiling too, so I knew she was just crying to say good-bye. That's what she always did. "When we sell the farm, May, I'll send you your share."

"You don't have to do that, Mama," May said. "You'll need it. You are gonna buy a house in Hachita, ain't you, or at least Lordsburg?"

Mama squinted at her. "I haven't made up my mind exactly where I'm gonna live, honey. It won't be Hachita, though. I can tell you that right now."

We were all out by the pickup. May and I got into the cab, and Mama waved and went back into the house with Rita and Trinket. Lance and Uncle Sean were standing by May's door.

"You take care," Uncle Sean said, slapping the top of the pickup, and Lance looked into her side, looking like he was about to cry. "I'll make Will take me to visit you on the ranch, May. I'm really gonna miss you, you know that? You've been great to me."

May suddenly reached out through the passenger side window and hugged Lance awkwardly. "I'm gonna miss you, too! You'll take care of Will, won't you, since he won't have me around?"

When May let him loose, he was sure enough crying. "I will, May."

Then he and Uncle Sean turned and walked together back into the house.

It was weird to me to see the two of them together and, again, I took myself out of the picture and tried to imagine that they were boyfriends. This time it hurt a little to think about that.

So May and I talked all the way to the Snow ranch. Mainly, May told me about Kelsey after all this time of being secretive, even though she knew I knew what was what.

Kelsey was a few years older than May and, according to May, her parents made her work off the ranch, to get a notion of what it was like to try to make it on wages. "They told her they weren't paying her way to go to college, either," May said, after a while.

"That was kind of mean, don't you think?" I asked. "Their only child?"

But May just laughed. "Kelsey could've cared less about that, Will. She said that when her parents die and she takes over the ranch, she's not going to run cattle."

Then May went into the plans she and Kelsey had for turning part of the ranch into a resort. It all sounded neat, but I wondered just how long it was going to be before Kelsey's parents did pass on.

When we arrived at the ranch headquarters, which sits just on the other side of the Peloncillos in a small valley surrounded by pines, the change in the scenery from desert to forest is breath-taking. Though that's how it is in this part of the country. I could tell that, at one time, the ranch was a big operation because there was a bunk house for the cowboys up on the side of a hill, as well as two or three small houses where I figured the foremen and their families had once lived. The main house was huge and rambling and was surrounded by old trees that looked about as tired as the fences and rock walls that had fallen in places.

Still it was beautiful and, as we drew near on a well-graveled road, May was becoming excited.

"It's one hell of a drive into Hachita from here, May," I said. "How does Kelsey do it?"

"Oh she doesn't live here, Will. We're renting an apartment in Lordsburg. But this is where I'm going to store my stuff."

"Ain't that gonna look kind of suspicious to her parents, though?"

May shook her head and sat up in the seat. She instructed me to drive past the main house and to pull up in front of a small wooden cabin. Smoke was curling out of the metal chimney pipe on the side of the house, and when I killed the engine, Kelsey came out of the cabin. She was dressed like a cowboy in boots and Levi's and a cowboy hat. The only thing that gave her away as being a woman was her breasts, which filled out the western-cut shirt.

I stayed in the pickup, while May got out. May was wearing Levi's, as well, and a pullover sweatshirt, but there was no mistaking her for a man with her long red hair, which shone suddenly in a ray of sunlight peeking through a split-topped pine. Then she was in shadow as she stepped onto the porch. They kissed right in front of me, and I didn't even have time to look away, in case they thought I was spying.

I looked back toward the main house and saw that they could have been running around naked and nobody would have seen them from here. The cabin was a little downhill from the main house and surrounded by shrubs and pines.

When they finished kissing, May came and got me out of the pickup and introduced me to Kelsey. We knew each other, but had rarely talked.

"May's got a soft spot for you, Will," Kelsey said, smiling. "You and your little boyfriend."

"Yeah, well she's my favorite sister, too," I said, wondering why I had put it exactly like that, because I loved all my sisters, just in different ways.

"It's probably because you and May have more things in common," Kelsey said. "We'll get your things unloaded in a minute, honey," Kelsey said to May. Then she turned back to me. "Might as well come on in and have a cup of hot chocolate, Will. It gets a lot colder on this side of the continental divide, and this high up. We've already had snow."

It was like being in a western as the sun went down, and Kelsey stoked a fire in a wood-burning stove. The cabin was mainly one big room, with a couple of doors leading off to what I bet was a bedroom and a bathroom. Still it was kind of rustic and neat, and Kelsey told me that this is where she lived when she didn't have to be at work for a few days. I told her it was neat, and she retorted that I'd freeze my butt off at night, because the only heat in the cabin was the wood stove. But it was hot in there, and when I finally left, it was well after dark. I wanted to get back home, figuring everybody had already eaten supper.

* * *

So I got home a little after eight o'clock. When I drove up, I expected Uncle Sean's car to be in the drive and everybody to be in the living room watching television. But his car was gone.

When I went inside, Mama, Rita, and Trinket were sitting at the kitchen table working a jigsaw puzzle. Mama's cigarette smoke filled the air above their heads like a cloud, and I could tell she'd been chain-smoking.

I asked where Uncle Sean was, and Trinket said he and Lance had gone off somewhere.

I tried to act like it didn't bother me, but all of a sudden I had a weird feeling in the pit of my stomach. It wasn't that I didn't trust both Uncle Sean and Lance. It was just a sudden thought, like those I had been having, imagining that Lance would find Uncle Sean as pretty as I did, and Uncle Sean would think that Lance was as beautiful as I did, too. And maybe they had feelings for each other.

I ate a quick sandwich and watched Mama and the girls working the puzzle, trying not to act upset, then I went to my room and got caught up on writing in this journal. That's where I've been now since I got home. I have to take snatches of time like this to put things down. But as we haven't been doing any farm work now for a while, I have more time. Sometimes, though, maybe it's too much time to think and write. I've read over what I just wrote and right away I see that I don't need to worry about Lance and Uncle Sean, because Uncle Sean has always been honorable, and he knows what it feels like to be cheated on by somebody he loves. And Lance and I just put on wedding bands that says we're married like those guys Uncle Sean and I saw in Deming that time.

* * *

I must've fallen asleep, because Lance woke me up trying to undress me in the dark. I was lying on top of the covers and felt the spiral notebook under my right shoulder. I was cold and Lance was shivering, having already undressed.

"What happened, Will? How come you're not in bed?" he said, kind of whispering, though we were at the other end of the house from everybody. When I finally came awake, a surge of anger jolted me. "Just writing, Lance. Where were you, anyway? How come you and Uncle Sean went out? You could've waited for me!" Images were going through my mind and I tried to shake them off.

"Huh?" Lance said, as I sat up. I was glaring at him, but luckily he couldn't see me in the dark. I tried to calm down.

"You and Uncle Sean," I said, whispering, myself. "How come you didn't wait for me? Where did you go?"

When I was undressed, we both hurried under the covers and automatically wrapped our arms around each other.

"We didn't know how long you were going to be, Will, and it seemed like a good time for him and me to get to know each other, better."

"And did you?"

"What d'you mean, Angel?"

I could hear the innocence in his voice, and I knew without having to go any further that I was being stupid. "You know, really get acquainted. I've told you so much about him, and him about you. Did you hit it off?"

Lance laughed softly. "Don't even think what you're thinking. We drove up to Lordsburg and ate in that old restaurant. You know, Kranberry's?"

"Umhmmm."

"It was his idea. I guess he wanted to know if I was good enough for you, because he sure grilled the hell out of me. What was I planning to do when I graduated? Did I love you? Did I think I could stay committed to you?"

"He asked all those kinds of questions?"

"Yeah, Angel. He did. He doesn't want to ever see you get hurt. He said you were too good of a man, that you deserved the best."

I began to feel guilty ever worrying a single instant about Lance and Uncle Sean, and I was again glad he couldn't see my face, because I'm sure it was red as a beet.

"Did he tell you about himself?"

Lance laughed again, a little more loudly. "Oh, yeah, after he told me how you were always trying to get him to kiss you and get into bed naked with him. He said you scared him to death when he was here back when you were fourteen."

Tears leaked out onto my face and I wiped them away. Uncle Sean had tried to tell me how dangerous my love for him was, and he had remembered these past years.

Lance rolled over on top of me, and I could feel that he was stiff. He began kissing my face, and I kissed back. Then he propped himself up on my chest, kind of pushing himself between my legs with his little buddy, which wasn't so little at the moment.

"But I feel so sorry for him, Angel."

"He told you more about Theodore Seabrook?"

"Yes, and about his last boyfriend, only a lot more than he told us the other day. He says he doesn't belong anywhere. He doesn't like how flighty and over-sexed most men are. He says he just wants to find one man to love and who loves him."

I didn't say anything, because I knew that's what Uncle Sean wanted. Like Lance, I felt sorry for him. Lance didn't say anything for a minute, either. And then we made love, as desperately and as wildly as we always did. In a way, it was sad, because I was thinking of Uncle Sean down the hall in May's room, lying there alone, and I think it was on Lance's mind, too, because we were both crying.

* * *

The next day, I got up still feeling guilty about the unfair thoughts that had been running through my head, and I swore I'd never lose trust in Lance or Uncle Sean again. I also kept sighing with relief that I hadn't made any accusations, because for all the trouble Lance and I had gone through this past few months at school, we'd never had a real fight.

So at breakfast, I was thinking just how little time there was to be with Uncle Sean. It was the 29th day of December, and he was leaving on New Year's Day. I couldn't just let that precious time slip by. Only I didn't have any idea what we should do, and when

Lance suggested that Uncle Sean meet Dick and Casey, I couldn't see anything wrong with it.

When school's out for the holidays, most kids old enough to work on the ranches and farms put in hard days. After the harvest is done, the rest of the winter is spent clearing the land of the cotton, grain, and corn stalks. Come January, it's time to break-plow the land. So Lance, Uncle Sean, and I drove over to Cotton City to find Casey. I knew it wouldn't be a good idea for us to drive out to his farm, since he'd said his family didn't want him to be seen with me. So I was going to call him from the Cotton City Market, but who should I run into but Rick Zumwalt. He was coming out of the market and I was right by the door in the phone booth.

"What the fuck are you doing here, faggot?"

He put it just like that. I didn't expect him to be friendly, now that he and Rita had broken up. But his attack kind of took me by surprise, anyway. I had the phone to my ear and someone on the other end picked up, just as Rick spoke.

Before I thought, I asked for Casey, and Rick heard me. He grabbed the phone out of my hand, glaring at me. "You leave my kid brother alone," he said, brandishing the phone in a fist, like a club.

A second later, Uncle Sean came up behind Rick and put him in a choke hold. I didn't even know he'd seen what was happening.

Rick elbowed backwards, but Uncle Sean was too quick, and pulled Rick off balance, so he couldn't gain leverage, and held him like that, Rick flailing, but tough as steel. I'd forgotten that Uncle Sean was strong and had probably learned some of his moves in the army. Still, he was straining against Rick's heavier weight.

"Let him go, Uncle Sean," I said, refusing to back down. Rick had dropped the phone when Uncle Sean got him. It was dangling in the booth. I listened on the receiver, but the line was dead.

Uncle Sean was ready for Rick when he dropped him, stepping back as Rick fell to the ground then sprang to his feet in the next instant, turning and swinging his fists. That's when I tackled Rick from behind, forcing him to the ground.

"There's three of us, Rick," I said. Lance was standing by the car a few feet away, looking angry. "Why don't you just cool your heels?"

Rick bucked me off and took a swing, catching me on the chin. It felt like I'd been hit with a baseball bat, and just as Uncle Sean was jumping into the middle of Rick, a pickup skidded to a halt and Casey jumped out and smashed into Rick, knocking him to the ground a second time. This time he stayed down, looking up at the three of us.

"I get it now," he said, nodding and spitting off to the side. "You..." he jabbed a finger at me, "and you..." he said, jabbing the air again at Uncle Sean, "and you, little brother. You're all fucking faggots. And you better watch your backs."

"What do you call yourself, Rick?" I asked, feeling like my jaw was dislocated, because it hurt to just open my mouth. "You beat up my sister and your brother. You gonna turn into a wife beater like your father?"

Rick just lowered his head as he got up deliberately and slowly from the ground, reminding me of the stance a bull out in the pasture sometimes takes, about to charge. Only I think the fight had been knocked out of him.

"You've done gone too far now, Barnett. You just insulted my family, and I'm going to let all my brothers and my father know it." Then he looked at Casey. "And if you're loyal to family, you better get the fuck away from them, right now. I'll tend to you later."

I shouldn't have let my anger get to me. I should have kept my mouth shut about Rick beating up Casey, and I should've never said anything about his father being a wife beater. I was shaking when Rick walked away, dusting himself off. The hunch of his back, the way he swaggered and got into his pickup, then looking back at the four of us—I knew there would be trouble, so I turned to Casey.

"Hey, man, listen. Rick started this. We just stopped in town to call you."

Casey was ashen-faced, glancing back over his shoulder at the sound of Rick's pickup peeling out of the grocery store lot. Then he looked at me. "What was that remark about my father? You just stepped into a pile of it, Will. Rick ain't gonna forget, and he will tell Dad."

I tried to apologize, but Casey had already turned and stomped off, just like his brother, and I didn't know if he was angry with me or Rick.

So, we nixed the idea of trying to find Dick. Casey was out, and none of us felt like doing anything. So we all got back into Uncle Sean's car. We were silent as we sat there, Lance between me and Uncle Sean.

"What was that all about?" Uncle Sean finally said. "One minute you're on the phone, and the next this goon comes out of the store and acts like he's going to brain you."

My jaw still hurt, and Lance had kissed it several times, his violet eyes going a darker shade at his concern. "Tell him," Lance said.

So, as we were leaving Cotton City, I told Uncle Sean about how Rick was the one who started everybody talking about me and Lance, and how Lance was attacked after the football game, and how Rick had beat up Casey and later, Rita, when she broke up with him.

"Then it's a good thing you're selling out and moving on," Uncle Sean said. "Sounds like there's always going to be bad blood between your families. Besides, Will, this isn't any place to live, even if everybody got along."

We were already past Animus and had turned east toward Hachita. At his remark, I looked out the window at the rolling hills, the rocky sides of the little Hatchet Mountain coming up in the distance, the barren landscape, catching the gleam of the newly built smelter that would one day spill its smoke into the sky. It was a further scar on the land, just as the ore mining had been earlier in the century that left deep gashes in the sides of the mountains, and turn-of-the-century garbage from the miners strewn wherever they had lived.

Still, a lump formed in my throat to know that we would all be moving away, leaving behind a small trace of our own lives from the farm that Daddy had started, and knowing that his ashes were an inseparable part of the earth he had tilled.

* * *

So we didn't get to introduce Uncle Sean to Dick Lamb or Casey Zumwalt. Instead, Uncle Sean invited Mama and the girls to go along and we all loaded into his '57 Chevy, which still ran like a race horse, and we headed into Deming and took in a movie. We ate at a steak house between Deming and Common, called the Angus Iron, and talked about the future. It was too bad that May wasn't with us, so I told them all what she and Kelsey were planning to do with the ranch, once Kelsey inherited it, telling them about all the neat buildings at the headquarters.

Mama's eyes grew bright with tears as I was telling them that. Maybe part of it was happiness for May, knowing that she would probably make a go of it on the ranch, since she was good with her hands, but part of what brightened Mama's eyes was probably also her realization that May was like me. Why else would she be settling in with a woman?

Rita wouldn't graduate from Animas High, but she said she was glad. Anywhere would be better. Trinket wanted to move to a real city, not because she was dazzled with the thought of all the people, but she already knew she needed to get good grades in a good high school so she could get into a good university. I heard Uncle Sean's influence there and smiled at my little sister. If she did become a vet, I could just see her handling large dogs that probably outweighed her.

It would have been a good end to what had started out as a lousy day, with the fight with Rick Zumwalt, but as soon as we walked into the door at home, the phone was ringing and ringing and didn't stop until Mama answered it. It was close to midnight, and a call that late at night couldn't be good.

While Mama was on the phone, the look on her face getting worse and worse, I made coffee, and Rita and Trinket cleaned up a few dirty dishes. All of us stayed busy, waiting for Mama to get off the phone. I knew she was talking to Margie Collins. Margie was as good as the ten o'clock news. How she found out things, I'll never know, unless in her boredom with her life, she stayed on the phone day and night.

It was late and Mama sent Trinket off to bed. She had gone pale and had reached for her pack of cigarettes about halfway through the conversation with Margie. When she got off the phone a few minutes later, she had smoked three cigarettes to the filter. She had Rita stay with us, though, so I figured it had something to do with Rick. I kept regretting the remark I had made to him that morning in the parking lot of the Cotton City Market; and I kept thinking something must have gone horribly wrong. I was afraid Casey had been beat up again.

By the time Mama came to the table, Uncle Sean, Lance, Rita, and I were sitting silently, with our coffee untouched in the mugs, all our eyes on her.

She lit another cigarette, her eyes looking kind of wild, and my heart was thudding. I couldn't imagine what it was. Mama's hands were shaking. "That kid you're friends with, Will...Casey?"

I nodded, suddenly feeling very afraid. "What, Mama?"

"He just killed his brother Rick and his father."

Rita's intake of breath was so loud, I could almost feel my own being sucked out of me. I glanced at Rita and saw the pain in her face, the tears almost immediately pooling then sliding down her cheeks. Lance and I exchanged glances, both of us looking stunned, I guess. At least Lance's face reflected how I felt. Uncle Sean looked troubled, since we'd told him how Casey had been treated in that family. He was the only one still calm enough to ask Mama what had happened.

All I could think was it was my fault, and my words about Rick being a wife beater like his father came pounding back in my ears as if I had just spoken them.

Mama related the news that some sort of family argument broke out there at the Zumwalts, "and they said that Casey came out of nowhere all of a sudden with his deer rifle and shot his father, first, and then turned it on Rick. Casey's in jail in Lordsburg," Mama said, mashing out the cigarette in the ashtray. She folded her hands together, as if she didn't know what to do with them, and finally grew silent.

In fact, all of us were. There wasn't anything to do, but I felt like there ought to be.

"Well, what did Margie say, Mama?" I asked. "Didn't she have any idea what happened—or what they were fighting about?"

Mama shook her head. "I don't know, Will. She didn't know, though she knows as well as I do what a mean bastard Mr. Zumwalt is. He's always been hard on his boys and cruel to his wife."

* * *

I was too stunned to sleep, and so was Lance. We lay there for at least an hour, silent, holding each other, every once in a while commenting on Casey and the way he'd been beaten. "I know how he felt," Lance said. "I was this close a hundred times to killing my stepfather, and if I'd had a gun I probably would have."

"But if I just hadn't said that to Rick, about his father being a wife beater, don't—"

"It's not your fault, Angel," Lance said, putting his hand over my mouth in the dark, as if shutting me up would change things. It was true, though. I did say too much, and had gotten Casey in trouble. Somebody like Rick wasn't going to let it go, and now he was dead, no telling what kind of beating they'd given Casey before he shot them. I could imagine that it was even worse than the beating he'd been given before.

I must've fallen asleep, because when dawn came creeping gray and the wind rattled the window, I opened my eyes, at first wondering why I felt so sad, until it all came rushing back. Casey was in jail for killing Rick and his father.

Casey was in big trouble, and it was my fault. And there wasn't anything I could do about it.

Except that when Lance and I met Uncle Sean in the kitchen and we toyed with our eggs and bacon, he suggested that we drive up to Lordsburg to see if we could get in to talk to Casey.

It was a cold morning, and the wind was high, blowing sand across the highway from the west like snow, forming snaking patterns that broke up as we drove through. The sky was a light brown where the dust had risen like clouds. The mountains to the west were invisible behind the wall of dust. The wind buffeted the car as we drove. Inside all of us were quiet, lost in our own thoughts. Mine were on Casey, and it's odd that all I could see was me knocking him down during football practice, and his face a mass of bruises from the beating Rick had given him, as if I had given him the bruises, just like I had gotten him in trouble with Rick.

Lance and I held hands there in Uncle Sean's car, and Uncle Sean kept his right arm across the seat back as he drove, laying a hand on my shoulder and squeezing it sometimes, just like in the old days when he and I were working the farm; only now, I didn't feel turned on at his touch like I used to, just felt that he was doing his best to comfort me.

When we got out at the Hidalgo County Jail, the wind had shifted and came out of the north, cold as ice and full of grit. I was crying and could barely see as we went up the stone steps and entered the brick façade building, our footsteps echoing off the tile floor. Then Uncle Sean took over at the desk, asking if we could see Casey.

"Your business?" the cop behind the desk asked, his voice as cold as the wind. He looked up at the three of us.

"We're friends," I said, drying my eyes, and feeling my nose was runny, which I wiped on the sleeve of my jacket. "He and I play football together."

"Don't matter," the cop said. "You gotta be family or his court-appointed attorney."

"Can't you give him just five minutes?" Uncle Sean asked.

"To do what?" the cop persisted. "You ain't family or his attorney, what good's it going to do?"

But Uncle Sean wasn't taking 'no' for an answer. "They're friends, man. The kid in there's a minor, probably scared out of his mind. At least let him see one friendly face."

The cop turned away and pushed a button on the console behind him. "Just him," he said, cocking his head at me. "Five minutes, and you be outta there. Otherwise I get in trouble."

So a minute later, I was sitting in a chair on the other side of the cell. Casey was crying his eyes out. He looked as bad as the morning he showed up at school, with his face a bloody mess, again, and he looked as small as I'd ever seen him, as if he'd shrunk six inches, looking more like a kid than a seventeen year old. He was wearing an orange jumper and paper shoes, and it was cold as hell, and he kept shivering as he sat in his chair on the other side. When he put his hands on the bars, I folded mine around them, feeling how cold his fingers were. I could feel him shaking through his hands, and I knew he was scared and cold and probably in for it.

"It's my fault, Casey. If I hadn't said that to Rick. You were right. We shouldn't have come looking for you there in Cotton City. I knew you weren't supposed to be seeing me and Lance. I'm sorry."

"It ain't your goddamned fault, Will. You spoke true, what you said." Casey's lips were so bruised and puffy it sounded like he'd said, *"You smoked roo,"* which almost made me start crying again, only I didn't want Casey to see it.

"What happened?"

Casey wiped tears off his face, wincing at the pain. "I couldn't take it anymore! Wickactin all hut, n'he's the one went'n told." Snot came out of Casey's nose, hanging off his upper lip, his eyes bloodshot, and one of them swollen shut.

"You seen a lawyer yet?"

He shook his head. "Not 'till Monday." He wiped the snot away with his sleeve, streaking his face. It glistened under the light.

"What's your mother saying? Or Stephen? Anybody on your side?"

"I don't know, Will. Somebody called the cops, and I was taken away. Mom was crying, Stephen was crying. Family was coming in, once word got out."

There wasn't anything I could do, I realized, not even now, except maybe tell them in court how his brothers had raped him and thrown him off the barn, like he was a ball to catch, how his father horse-whipped him, how Rick had beat him up.

Only at that moment, with the wind howling past the small barred window high up in the cell, and Casey hanging onto the bars with my hands wrapped around his, and both of us looking at each other and crying, it all seemed pretty hopeless.

"You want me to tell Dick anything?" I asked. "Does he know?"

Casey shrugged. "Don't know. Tell him, though."

"Anything else you want me to tell him?"

He shook his head. "Naw."

So a minute later, I left, wishing I could hug him tight and feeling like a creep just turning my back on him and walking out, him still hanging onto the bars.

# Part Three
# Coming to an End

## Fourteen
## What it Meant to Graduate

I graduated right on schedule in May of 1973. My graduating class consisted of thirty-nine students. For a small school, we have our share of local funding, and the ranchers of the county have formed a trust that provides scholarships to those whose academic achievements warrant recognition. That's kind of taken out of the letter I received announcing I was being given a scholarship. I hadn't expected it, until I remembered Mrs. Hendricks and Mrs. Blackmon had taken such an interest in me mid-freshman year when I wrote that essay about Daddy. And since that time, I had soared in writing and in the rest of my studies. I'll never really know how I made it, though, with school, running the farm without Daddy, and handling the problems Lance and I had with a few people. So, when I had taken my last class and walked up on stage to receive my diploma, and then woke up the next day, I felt as light as a feather. I had nothing to do, not a single book to crack, not a single weed to chop or tractor to hitch a plow to. Nothing, that is, until we had to get the farm ready to sell to Old Man Hill. My next step was college—only I had decided to wait until Lance graduated, which meant I'd put off starting school until January 1974. That was all right with me, because I needed time to gather up the tools and equipment and get it ready for auction, and help Mama load up a lifetime of things she didn't want to take with her when she moved. She either gave the stuff to the more needy families, sold it in yard sales, or I hauled it off to the dump.

Then in December of 1973, Lance graduated, and the same trust fund provided a scholarship for him as well. But this one came through because of the efforts of his art teacher, Mr. Drummond.

And there was the problem. His scholarship specifically named the Academy of Art College in San Francisco he was to attend, and if he didn't, his scholarship would be given to someone else. I had applied to and been accepted by the University of Texas at Austin, since Austin is where Uncle Sean was now living, and he wanted Lance and me to come out there. Lance said he didn't care about his scholarship. He wanted to move to Austin with me. I was torn, because I knew how talented he was, and I didn't want him to have to give up art school. We both cried about our dilemma, we loved each other so much. So rather than being happy, now that we both had our high school diplomas and had our whole future ahead of us, we faced having to live separately for awhile. To tell you the truth, I couldn't stand the thought of being without Lance for two years, which was the term of his scholarship. Thereafter, he was free to finish his bachelor's anywhere he wanted.

As we had been expecting, Mama sold the farm in July to Goddard Hill, and he gave us five-hundred dollars an acre, which he said was twice its value, and he gave us ten-thousand dollars for the house, barn, and well. We had auctioned off the old farm equipment and it had brought in a couple thousand more. So we would walk away with quite a bit more than Daddy had paid for the land thirty years before. Mama insisted on dividing up the money, because we were scattering to the four winds, though that wasn't quite true. Only May was going to be left behind, here in this part of the country, though she did seem happy. Uncle Sean had found Mama a house there in the hill country of Texas, not too far from Austin, where she and Trinket and Rita were going to live.

When Mama and Uncle Sean were talking about the house, I could hear the excitement in her voice. In fact, it was the lightest, happiest conversation she and Uncle Sean had had for a long time. When she got off the phone she was still beaming and told us the house Uncle Sean had found was a lot like the one he and Mama had grown up in there in Louisiana.

"It's a two-story with a steep roof. An attic bedroom for you," she said to Trinket. "You can finally have your own place to spread all your stuff out in. Sean says it's a fancy style with a wrap-around porch with pillars. There's even a chandelier in the dining room."

I was glad for Mama and figured it would be a good place for her to grow old in. It also sat on nearly forty acres of hill country with trees, grass meadows, and even a creek running through it. So I was happy for my family.

But all of us were leaving with a cloud over our heads. With Casey's trial that came up in February of 1973, a whole lot of things came out, which embarrassed Mama, who sat beside Margie Collins day after day during the trial. Only it wasn't really a trial with a jury, like you'd think, since Casey was a minor. It was just a couple of lawyers, the judge, and just about everybody who was anybody in Cotton City and folks from the rest of the county who came to gawk and whisper and hear the testimony.

I have to hand it to Margie Collins. She didn't take Rick's side at all. Like Mama, she had knowledge you wouldn't know she had, because she did keep some things to herself until the trial. And even when she was asked to tell what she knew about the family, she was reluctant to let it out. One bit of information that went in Casey's favor was that Mr. Zumwalt was a wife beater and just about everybody in Cotton City knew that he abused his children. Even Stephen, Casey's brother, who was just a year older than Casey, testified as to how his father had picked on Casey more than the rest of them.

And when I got to speak, I told them about the first time I had seen Casey beat up, and how it was Rick and his father who had done it. But lawyers sure are cold fish. I was practically crying having to tell about it, but they hardly even blinked.

The thing that might've swayed the judge in Casey's favor was the doctor's records, showing that Casey had a history of broken bones that had never been satisfactorily explained to the doctor. Just like the rest of the boys. So in the end, Casey was let go.

But it didn't really help him. He went down in school after the trial. He quit sports and never was the same. Kids were okay around him, but they shied away from him anyway, and he felt it, I guess. Since he was a year behind me, I only saw him in school for the last half of the spring semester of 1973. He never would do anything with me or Lance, and he and Dick went their separate ways as well.

I had visited with Dick on the day I went to the jail to see Casey. At first, he seemed like he was okay with what had happened, and talked about him and Casey still being best buddies. What I didn't hear from him or Casey was the word 'love.' And I figured what they had was just convenient sex, both of them experimenting, both of them trying to pretend for awhile that they were like me and Lance.

Dick graduated with me, and the last I heard that summer was that he had headed for the coast in his pickup, with a few hundred bucks in his pocket and an urge to explore the gay world.

Then Lance graduated in December of 1973, and like I said, we'd already sold the farm, so it was just a matter of what he and I were going to do about going to separate schools. I wanted him to make a fair decision, though I was about to die that he'd choose to go to that art school there in San Francisco.

So on the day after Christmas of 1973, he and I took off up to the rocky ledge overlooking the Phelps-Dodge smelter plant where we had first met.

It was a cold-as-ice kind of day, with the wind blowing from the west. Lance was looking really good. He'd taken to wearing a cowboy hat, and I had gotten him a sissy-colored lavender sweater with a rolled collar that hugged his body and showed off all his newly formed pecks and abs, and made me jealous that I couldn't be the sweater. More beautiful than ever, with the sweater bringing out the violet in his eyes and complementing the tanned skin tones of his face, he sat down on the rocky ledge, hugging his knees. I sat down next to him, on the same side I had sat that day I first laid eyes on him, hugging my knees as well. I was wearing a hooded sweat shirt and over that I was wearing my letter jacket and a cap. Still it was cold, but I was shaking more from what we were trying to decide.

We both looked out over the smelter plant, glinting brightly in the sun, both of us shivering with the hard cold of the desert wind moaning through the grease-wood on the rocky hill behind us.

We were both wearing our rings. We had never taken them off, even when it meant showing up at school with them on. People had noticed, and some of the students had made cutting remarks, trying to embarrass us. By then, with all the razzing Lance and I had been through with Casey and Dick, and the trouble with Rick Zumwalt, and the trial, a few remarks just didn't faze me or Lance. But even that seemed in the distant past, now that we had both graduated and, like I said, had our whole future ahead of us.

"You going to tell your mother you're leaving?" I asked, because it seemed appropriate, now that we were looking down on the smelter plant.

"Hell the fuck no!" Lance said, frowning at me, and even now making me cringe with the force of his language. "Why'd you even ask that, Will? She's dead, dead, dead, as far as I'm concerned!"

"I just thought—"

"Well don't," he said, cutting me off, hurting my feelings. "You're my family, now."

We stared out over the rolling away hills and mountains to the west for a moment longer, then Lance got up. "This isn't working, Angel. It's too fucking cold!"

He was angry, and it was just coming out, now. I tried to realize that he was trying to handle things, all sorts of things, like leaving without saying good-bye to his mother, but more importantly, coming to a decision if he was going to go to the school in San Francisco and us being separated for at least two years.

I shivered again and stood up, too. I tried to wrap my arms around him and kiss him, but he turned his face away. "If you do that, Will, I won't be able to make a rational decision."

Again, I felt my face sting with hurt, but it was silly. I knew it wasn't me he was angry with but our situation.

His classes at the art school started in two weeks, so if he decided to go, we had to get him packed and drive him out there. He'd already been accepted, since we had carried through with the application, regardless of whether he decided he would really go. The professors had written back after getting a look at his portfolio, practically begging him to come. And I knew they were right, and that the best decision for Lance would be to go.

So we stood there, both shivering, looking at each other; me on the verge of tears, wanting to hold him, but knowing it would be all the more difficult for him to decide. We'd both agreed that we would have to make a decision today, and had agreed that we would come here and think it through. So far, however, we had only aggravated each other.

I took his hand, which he let me hold, and led him back to the pickup. We got in and sat as far apart as we could. Although the wind was howling past ferociously, it was almost warm and cozy in the cab.

"If I go," Lance said, looking over at me with tears in his eyes, "you promise me you won't go find yourself another husband?"

I could hardly speak, because I knew he had made a decision. "Of course I won't, Lance. I love you so much it hurts! And if you go, will you promise the same thing? You're a knockout and, there in San Francisco, you'll have guys hitting on you all the time. You'll probably find someone who's ten times better looking than this old farmer."

Lance snorted a laugh, which ended in a sob. "That's impossible, Angel. And you're no old farmer."

"Then you've decided?" I could feel a sob starting way down in my chest, and I took a deep breath trying to keep it from coming up.

He nodded, looking over at me with tears beginning to spill out. "You think I'm good enough to be a real artist?"

I nodded as well, fighting the sob welling up. "You are. You deserve this. I'll be waiting for you, Lance. I'll save up all my love milk and when we see each other I'll fill you up."

"And I'll do the same! I promise!"

And with that decided, we just ripped our clothes off. It was like we'd already been apart for months, the way we went at it. When we were spent, the windows were steamed up, our lips were bleeding, our little buddies were raw, and the cab of the pickup smelled heavenly with the scent of our love making.

Then Lance dared me to step out of the pickup, naked, into the cold wind. Which we did. We stood together overlooking the sweeping away of the land, down on the smelter plant, and Lance took my hand and we raised our arms.

"Piss on you!" Lance screamed at the top of his lungs, and he started pissing into the wind.

"Piss on you!" I screamed, about to laugh, feeling nutty as a fruitcake. But I knew what Lance was doing, and I let go with a stream of piss, as well. We were pissing on his parents and defying the world, and we were doing it together. Always together.

The wind blew our water back on us, wetting our legs, leaving my skin feeling as if it had been hit with ice water.

But we danced around naked for a minute or two until we were both about to freeze our peckers off and ran back to the pickup, hugging and laughing and crying.

# *Fifteen*
# *The Separation*

According to the road atlas, it was just a little over a thousand miles from Hachita to San Francisco. Lance and I were going to take three days to get there. We'd already put off taking the trip as long as we could, but when there was only five days left before he had to be at the Academy of Art College for the beginning of classes, we knew we had to leave. So we loaded up the pickup the night before we left, and I covered everything with a tarpaulin. We joked about us looking like the Beverly Hillbillies, and I guess that's exactly how I felt. I've never said much about the pickup, but Daddy always believed in buying the best, and he always thought that was Ford. It was a 1965 model with a v-8 engine and the standard four-speed transmission. He'd always taught me to change the oil and filter and plugs regularly and it had never given us a lick of trouble, but after almost nine years as a farm vehicle, it looked beat up and worn out. So on the day that we took off, I'd washed it (though it didn't do much good), changed the oil and everything, checked the belts, the transmission fluid. I'd already bought a new set of tires. So we were ready by four the morning we left.

Well, actually, we weren't ready at all. But we were sticking to the decision we'd made out on the rock ledge a few days before. Even Mama was surprised at the decision, and so were Trinket and

Rita, and Rita got me aside the night before when Lance was making sure he had everything packed.

"I don't know, Will. I don't think I'd be able to do it. You guys'll be almost two-thousand miles apart, and it won't be easy to see each other for a long time. That's halfway across the country."

I knew it, and even while she was telling me this, my heart was pounding and I had a sick feeling in my stomach.

"And you know what they say about time and distance," she continued. I knew she wasn't trying to be mean, because there were tears in her eyes and fear, too. I think she loved Lance and didn't want to see him lost to our family.

"They also say that absence makes the heart grow fonder," I said, realizing even as the words were out of my mouth, that they were hollow—a cliché. "I'm scared, too, Rita, but Lance needs this."

"He needs you!" she said. "And you need him. This is crazy."

I knew it was, too, and I went to bed that night with Lance feeling depressed. This would be the last time we spent in our bed. He pointed this out, then we reached for each other and made love, and cried holding each other, and fell asleep.

When we got up at four the next morning to leave, everybody got up to see us off. Trinket was crying and kept hugging Lance. Mama was crying, too. She always cried, but this time it was different. It was more than just saying good-bye. Lance had come into her life, she had learned to love him like a son, and now he was leaving. She wasn't ready to let him go. She was wearing her old blue terrycloth robe and looking older than I'd ever seen her. Her eyes were puffy from lack of sleep, so I figured she had lain awake all night.

She hugged Lance and kissed him on the cheek. "You got the money in a safe place, honey? You let Will pay for gas and motels and food. You hang onto what I gave you. Get a bank account as soon as you can. Eat at the school if it's cheaper. And if you need anything, you just call. You have Sean's number? He'll know our new telephone number and our address. Write often!"

Lance was nodding and fighting back tears, which made me fight back my own.

And then we were off into the predawn darkness. By the time I got back here, Mama and the girls were supposed to have everything packed into a U-Haul truck, and we'd all leave together for our trip to Austin. So this first trek of my trip with Lance was just one of driving solid for over a week, and I didn't know how I was going to handle it all. I wasn't afraid of the driving so much as what it would mean. I'd say good-bye to Lance in San Francisco and, no sooner than I arrived back home, it wouldn't be home anymore. By then, Mama, Trinket, Rita, and I would drive in a caravan to Texas.

Lance and I were silent, as the first twenty miles from the farm to Hachita passed beneath us. It was still dark when we headed up the highway, north to Lordsburg, and it was still dark, but kind of gray in the east, when we got onto Interstate 10. Lance turned around and looked for a long moment, as we left the string of lights of Lordsburg behind.

Then we made small talk, and Lance curled up against me. Neither of us talked about the separation from each other, but it was on my mind, with the constant hum of the tires on the smooth pavement, reeling out the miles beneath us, as if I might reach the end of the line and suddenly stop and tell him: This is crazy, Lance. We're heading in the wrong direction! But I didn't—couldn't—because he didn't say anything about it, so I figured that he thought it was best, too.

We stopped for gas and breakfast at a truck stop outside Tucson, Arizona. The sun was well up by then, but we were at a higher altitude, and it was a cold January morning, though bright and sunny. The clouds were just in my heart.

When Lance went off in search of a restroom, I watched him go, feeling tears sting my eyes. I had come to know his body, every inch, every curve, every mole and, yet, this morning he could have been a stranger I was admiring from a distance. He was wearing the lavender, rolled-neck sweater, Levi's, boots, and his cowboy hat, though his sandy brown hair was long enough to curl over the neck of the sweater. I glanced around the truck stop café watching some of the truckers watching Lance saunter across the room, then disappear down a short hallway. Above the entrance was a sign that said: RESTROOMS • SHOWERS.

So I wrote notes in my notebook, mainly things I remembered Rita saying to me, as well as how everyone reacted to our leaving, then glanced around the room. There was only one tired-looking waitress making the rounds. Some of the truckers tried to make small talk with her or flirt, but she didn't look to be in the mood and could hardly make her hard face reflect a smile. Lance returned to our table with a thin smile of his own, and a moment later the waitress came up to us.

She was smiling broadly, however, and leaned in close to the table. "Now aren't you two a sight for sore eyes."

I didn't know what she meant. "You're tired?"

"Been on my feet since midnight." She smiled again. "Where you headed?"

"We're—"

"I'm heading out to Frisco to art school," Lance said, cutting me off.

"Now ain't that sweet!" the waitress cooed. "But what's your wife think about that?"

Lance looked confused, but I realized the waitress had seen his wedding band. Then she noticed mine, which I didn't think to hide, and when our eyes met, something passed across her facc, a look of confusion, then a realization of sorts, and her smile snapped shut.

Her face hardened. "What'll it be?"

We ordered eggs and bacon and coffee.

"What was that all about?" Lance asked, when the waitress was out of earshot.

I touched my ring and nodded toward his, and understanding crossed his face.

"Oh!" He grinned. My heart throbbed at his beauty, and the depression lifted a little, so that when our breakfast arrived, I had a good appetite.

I tanked up on coffee while I studied the map and showed him the route I wanted to take. "If you don't mind, I'd like to cut northwest from Phoenix, up highway 93 to Kingman, spend the night there."

* * *

If anything, the country was more harsh than it was around Hachita, except for patches of green as we passed farms with what must've been winter wheat or barley. Lance was soon bored with the sameness of the landscape.

"Geez, Will, is the entire southwest just brown desert and rocky looking mountains?"

"I can't say," I said, kind of laughing at his dismay. "I've only been as far as Phoenix. At least we're crossing the Sonoran desert, now, instead of the Chihuahuan, like we have at home."

"There's a difference?"

"Some. They've got saguaro cactus and we've got yuccas and mesquite."

And so our conversation went as the miles passed—safe and trivial, avoiding the painful facts of why we were traveling toward San Francisco.

We had a late lunch on the south side of Phoenix. I was still jittery after driving through the outskirts of the city, my knuckles sore from gripping the wheel when we hit the heavy traffic. It was noticeably warmer, too, and we'd actually passed orange groves on the way. Both of us were amazed, though we were soon back in the desert as we came into the sprawl of Phoenix.

We stopped at another truck stop for gas and lunch. With each stop, I felt a little more depressed, realizing that three days was going to pass quickly, and I thought about telling him I didn't want him to do this.

Still, he said nothing, and we didn't talk about it.

"I love you, Will!" Lance said, suddenly, when we were back on the road, trying to find the turn off for Highway 93. "You won't forget that, will you?"

I looked over at him, and he was crying, if anything making him look more beautiful than ever, and I remembered that even the dark bruises and the gashes on his face from his stepfather's beatings couldn't hide his looks. "Of course I won't forget it. I hope you won't forget me, once you get settled there in Frisco. Uncle Sean says there's more gay men there than anywhere else in the whole country, and they're all out for sex."

Lance frowned. "Well, I'm not! I've had my fill of letting men paw me on the streets. Who needs that? If it weren't for this stupid art school, I wouldn't be going to Frisco at all. I'd be going with you and the rest of the family!"

I almost stopped the pickup right then, because it sounded like Lance was having strong doubts.

"But I guess I'll never amount to anything unless I do it. That's supposed to be one of the best schools in the country."

So I let my foot settle onto the gas pedal and took the exit off Interstate 10 to Highway 93 when it came up.

Kingman was a lot farther than I realized and it was dark as pitch when we were coming into town. We'd passed several dusty looking Arizona towns and I was tired. My gas pedal leg was stiff, and I was thinking how good it would be to find a motel. Traffic was not quite as heavy on this highway as it had been on the interstate, but semi-trucks still bore down on us from behind and roared past, sometimes startling me out of the daze I'd been in. Lance slept off and on, always against me, and I kept my arm around him, trying to absorb the feel of his body into mine, hoping I could bring back the feeling when he wasn't there. Then he was awake again, and instead of looking around, he pulled his hat off and laid it on the dash, then laid his head on my lap and began to nibble at my Levi's. I was instantly aroused, and I ran my fingers through his hair.

My crotch was getting warm from his breath, as he began to wrestle the buttons of my fly open with his teeth.

I was getting stiff, feeling his breath heat moisten my underwear. He was doing the whole thing with his mouth. My little buddy strained upward, and his mouth found it and he began sucking on me through my shorts.

"Don't waste it," I said, feeling myself getting close to spilling my milk.

"Ummm," was all he said.

* * *

It was cold enough, now that it was midnight, and our breath showed in the air as we got out of the pickup and went into the first decent looking motel we came to. It was something from another era, rather than one of the new, clean-looking Motel 6's. But the price for a single room seemed reasonable to me. Even though I had plenty of money, I was still trying to conserve, because I had no idea what we would run into once we got into San Francisco.

The lobby was dimly lit, and a rather greasy-haired old lady sagged behind the check-in counter, flipping through a magazine. She barely acknowledged us as we walked up and I asked for a room.

"One of your singles, please," I said.

She looked up at me, as if she just realized I was there. "It only has one bed."

"Okay," I said.

But she shook her head, looking me right in the eye. "No, sir, young man. I ain't a gonna rent you a single room with one bed. Not two men."

I was so surprised I looked right back at her. Lance was standing behind me, and I could almost feel his presence, and I saw myself as he and I must look to the old woman—a couple of young guys, traveling together. "Why can't you?" I asked, still stunned. "I don't understand."

By now the old woman seemed fully alert, and the look on her face reminded me of the waitress at the truck stop, frowning at me with such distaste, I wondered if we smelled bad. "Because this establishment doesn't condone sodomy. That's why."

"What's that?" I asked, feeling a knot of understanding and dread form in my guts.

On the wall behind the desk, I saw keys in little cubicles for the many empty rooms, the clutter of the paperwork on the counter below the boxes, and a calendar on another wall from some oil company. A clock above the calendar said it was two minutes after twelve.

"Thou shalt not lie with a man as with a woman," the old lady said. "Read your Bible. Now why don't you two just git before I call the cops?"

My legs had begun to shake. Never in my wildest imagination did I think we'd run into such trouble at a motel. I was too tired and too surprised with the old woman to even think to argue. I was also angry, but she looked serious and the last thing Lance and I needed was a run-in with cops.

* * *

So we found another motel on the other side of Kingman and this time Lance stayed in the pickup until I checked in. We carried everything into the motel room and ate across the highway at another truck stop. This time our waitress didn't even notice our rings, but I had been given a lot to think about from that first day of travel. I downed a mug of strong, bitter coffee, and Lance did the same.

What happened at the first motel reminded me of the way it slowly dawned on me about being gay when I was a kid, and then discovering that people, including my parents, had known about this thing long before I did. Worst of all, people always had their minds made up about homosexuality and it didn't matter where you went, people hated it. I'd seen that in Rick Zumwalt, and even in Dick and Casey at one time. And if you get right down to it, it was the very thought of homosexuality that had caused Casey's father to beat him up, and which ended up getting him killed.

Still, when the old lady had threatened to call the cops on us if we didn't leave, it left me breathless. There she was running a motel with a whole slew of empty rooms, and she wasn't willing to take our twenty-four dollars.

So Lance and I talked about how we should handle things, considering that people noticed our rings, or assumed we were exactly what we were when we attempted to check into a motel together. Lance surprised me, because he wasn't surprised at all, though maybe a little angry.

"Angel," he said, when the waitress was out of earshot, "I should have warned you about some hotels. In New Orleans, some of 'em even put up signs. No prostitutes, male or female."

"You're kidding!" I was flabbergasted, but he just laughed.

"N'awleans is the kind of place where prostitution is common. You just learn to rent rooms for an hour or two and which places will let you. Besides, how many straight guys would ever share a bed?"

Talk about being a Beverly Hillbilly, my jaw dropped at what he was telling me, just as it had with the old bag at the motel. "But it makes me mad," I said. "It ain't nobody's business. Do you think we should take off our rings? I don't want to."

He told me he didn't want to either. "It would be like it wasn't permanent, and for me it is, Will. Even if we're going to be apart for two years, I'm not gonna take my ring off. You're the best thing ever happened to me."

I felt the same way and told him. As we finished our meal and went back to the motel, I felt the time slipping away, again.

When we got up the next morning and were on the road, I was smothered with thoughts of how quickly our time together was melting away. And with each town we passed through, with each stop for gas, I became more sad.

We traveled west and a little south to Needles, and I was disappointed as we entered California. I'd never been there, but I'd always heard what a beautiful state it was. If anything it was dreary and dry and brown. Even if this was in the middle of winter, I figured California would look different. From Needles, we continued west on Interstate 40, with the semi-trucks and cars getting quicker and faster, making me nervous. Out of the rearview mirror, I could see the tarpaulin fluttering in the wind and I laughed at just how much more like a hillbilly we looked than most of the cars on the road.

Lance sat close to me wearing his cowboy hat and kept his hand on my thigh. We were so far from home we didn't really care what people must've thought as they passed us, some of them craning their necks to get a look at us, because it was obvious we were both guys, sitting close. But nobody did anything, because it seemed everybody was in a big hurry, passing us like we were standing still. We ate at another truck stop in Barstow, and we traveled on as night came again, and I drove until we came to Bakersfield, where we spent the second night.

We did our routine where Lance stayed in the pickup and I went in and rented a room with a double bed. On this second night, I was more depressed than ever, feeling a constant lump in my stomach, and Lance seemed to be drooping a little, too. We ate at a Denny's in silence, looking at each other sadly, knowing our time was growing short. He looked so beautiful to me, as always, still wearing the sissy-colored lavender sweater with the rolled neck, and in the bright lights of the restaurant, his violet eyes were almost like gems.

"You're going to have to fight off women and men," I said, a moment after sighing quietly to myself at his beauty.

"Me?" he said, smiling, his pink lips looking so luscious I wanted to lean across the table and kiss him. "You're the one, Angel. You'll have a whole bunch of boys creaming in their pants in every class you take."

And so our conversation went, with little substance, and a lot of silly talk. Many times, I wanted to ask him to forget his schooling, and we'd turn around right there and head home. But I figured he should be the one to change his mind. I'm sure he would have done whatever I asked, so I kept my mouth shut. Back in the motel, we undressed and without even talking about it, we got into the shower together. We'd only bathed together once, and that was the first night we'd ever slept with each other. So it was special for us to both want to be together as much as we could.

We soaped each other up and clung together as the hot water steamed up the glass enclosure of the shower. We smashed our lips together, each trying to devour the other. Then we dried each other off and with our little buddies standing out from our bodies, drinking in the warm air of the room, we fell onto the bed without turning back the covers or turning off the lights and made love every which way, and did it again. The whole time the lump was there in my stomach, full of dread.

We got up early the next morning, eating in the same Denny's before the sun came up. We had each changed into clean clothes, rearranged our suitcases, and were heading north up Highway 99 by the time the sun came up. My jaw dropped at all the farmland I saw around Bakersfield, miles and miles of it in every direction. It made even Cotton City farms look like little gardens in comparison, and I wondered why Daddy had tried to scratch out a living on the only farm in Hachita, surrounded by the desert. But here was a place I wouldn't have minded growing up. I might have even wanted to stay in farming. Even though it was winter, I could tell they raised a lot of crops. I was also awed by the farm equipment I saw pulled up against the barns, tractors that looked like giants and the wide multi-rowed sweeps they pulled behind them. Looking out on all this, I felt a little lighter, in a way, though the lump was still there.

I can't explain it, I felt lighter still as we passed through Fresno, California, and the scenery began to change a little, and the wealth of California became more obvious to me (the hillbilly from Hachita, New Mexico), I decided that our decision was right. Lance deserved this art schooling, thanks to Mr. Drummond, who had no doubt twisted a few arms to give the out-of-town kid one of the school's precious scholarships.

Lance was darned good at the paintings and drawings he did, and so, as we were traveling down the highway, I got him to go through the brochures the Academy of Art College had sent him. I kept one eye on the ever-thickening traffic of the highway and another on the pictures in the brochures. "You're gonna blow their socks off," I said, tapping a picture in the brochure, which must have been an example of a student's work. "You're already better than that, and if you do as Uncle Sean says and paint some nude men, you'll probably make a lot of money from the rich queers in Frisco."

Lance snuggled against me, tossing the brochures onto the dash. "You think so, huh?"

"I know it, Lance. Just stay focused on why you're there, and you'll do all right."

"I wish you were going to be there, though," he said, and I felt the lump in my stomach stir.

"I will be." I wrapped my right arm around his shoulders and hugged him to me, hard. Just think of me, and I'll be there."

Lance sniffled a little and wiped his nose. "Please, Will, please don't forget me!"

Tears stung my eyes. "That would be impossible."

* * *

I drove hard, trying to make it into San Francisco as soon as we could. I wanted to find a really neat hotel and dress up and take Lance to a great restaurant. I didn't care what it cost. It would be our last night together, and it had to be something we'd both remember, something to sustain us for the months and months that would have to pass before we got together again. I was startled to realize that by the time we saw each other again (unless I came out over a holiday) we'd be twenty-one years old. It seemed like forever until then, even though I was nineteen, now.

* * *

I never was sure when we got to San Francisco, because as we got close, we just entered this endless city of streets, stop lights, buildings, freeways, signs that said one town or another—all without end, until we were driving up and down these steep hills and I was fighting to keep from rolling backwards, or getting honked at at stop signs. It was late in the afternoon and everything was wet and gray and foggy, and even though the sun wasn't down (or at least I didn't think it was) it was impossible to tell since the sky was just a gray roil of nothingness.

Lights were on in the buildings, too. Through the water-dappled windshield, the red and green stoplights were distorted, and there were people everywhere.

Lance had the city map out and guided me through the streets until we came to Mason Street, and there, atop a large hill that looked out over the city, sat this gigantic building with a sign above it that read "Fairmont Hotel." Earlier, we had stopped for gas and I had asked the long-haired attendant who took my money with impossibly pale hands where a nice hotel was. "I want something nice to remember San Francisco by," I told him, and he mentioned the Fairmont.

I drove the pickup into the innards of a parking garage, which also amazed me to think that the city was so tightly packed they had to build such places. We moved as much of the stuff as we could from the back of the pickup into the cab and with our suitcases in hand, we headed into the hotel from the bowels of the garage, riding up to the lobby in an elevator. When the doors opened into the lobby, I was slack-jawed with surprise, and several times I had to shut my mouth, or risk stepping on my tongue. The lobby was probably the biggest inside space I'd ever seen, except maybe the cotton gin in Cotton City. But this place was brilliant with light from several chandeliers, each as tall as a house. They were dripping with thousands of raindrop-shaped glass, and beneath them the lobby seemed to go on in every direction, with rugs and carpet strips, interspersed with couches, marble-topped tables, over-stuffed chairs, and so much room, I couldn't take it all in at once.

People dressed in suits and evening gowns and dripping with jewelry filled the lobby, and men and women dressed in spiffy looking uniforms like our high school marching band wore (maybe) rushed around pushing carts full of luggage, or carrying trays of drinks and food, or conducting other business I couldn't even imagine.

But Lance seemed right at home as he led me through the crowd to one side of the lobby where other uniformed peopled waited behind a large and busy counter, which I figured was where we checked in. I also figured he had been in hotels like this in New Orleans with some of the men who had provided a room when he was hustling on the streets and knew what to do. So when it was my turn, I stepped up to the counter and found myself eye-to-eye with another impossibly pale-skinned man. Although he had long hair like many of the other men I had seen in the lobby, it was cut in what I can only describe as a woman's hairdo.

But his eyes smiled in a way that made me smile back with relief. "A room for two," I said, then waited for him to gather up some paper work.

"How long will you be a guest?" he asked, still smiling.

I told him we would be staying just that night. He finished filling out the information and, when I was told how much I owed for the room, I tried not to show surprise as I forked over the hundred-dollar bills, trying to keep Lance from noticing that my hands were shaking as I put my wallet away.

"Dinner is served until nine p.m.," the clerk said, then looked askance at me. "Coat and tie, only."

All I could think to say was thank you, and turned to leave, when he snapped his fingers and another uniformed man stepped up next to us. Lance picked up our suitcases. "We can manage," he said to the man, then he cocked his head at me, and I followed Lance as we walked back across the lobby to a bank of elevators.

We traveled up several floors and walked down these long halls with velvet wall paper and enough lights mounted to the walls every few feet to power the entire town of Hachita, and finally got settled into our room. By then it was dark out and I stood at the window overlooking the city. It was warm and stuffy in the room, but the view was indescribable. All I could think of was I sure would hate to be Santa Claus, looking out on all those lights, and the blackness of the bay, beyond. We were at the edge of the United States, and I knew beyond the bay was the Pacific Ocean. Lance and I were also at the edge of our being together, at least while he was attending school here, and that seemed darker and deeper and more frightening to me than the ocean.

I felt so far from home, so far removed from everything that was familiar, I caught myself crying a little, thinking I was going to leave Lance here, alone. But I did my best that night, as we dressed up in our suits and polished shoes and had dinner in the restaurant, to not let on to him that I was feeling frightened for him—and maybe even for us.

The dining room at the Fairmont was big enough to seat everyone in the entire town of Hachita. Every table had thick, white tablecloths, shimmering glassware, catching the gleam of glittering chandeliers. Again, everyone was dressed in suits—or maybe tuxedos, though I've never seen a tux to know the difference. The women's jewelry glittered under the lights, and all over the restaurant was the music of laughter, frightening me in a way when I looked across the table at Lance.

He belongs here, I thought. He was dressed in a black suit with a white shirt and a blue tie. I'd seen it in his closet, but had never thought before now about the circumstances in which he'd be wearing it—certainly not at a dinner in an expensive hotel on the edge of the continent, where he and I would be saying our good-byes. Looking around and back at Lance, I could tell that his was an expensive suit, and with his longish hair, freshly washed and also catching the bright lights, he actually looked at home here, while I felt like I stuck out like Jethro of "The Beverly Hillbillies" might. I was wearing one of Daddy's nice suits that Mama had thought to keep out for me, but my hair was its usual short-cut style, and I felt like a dressed up hayseed, which made me feel even worse.

When the waiter brought the menus, I opened it and thought I was reading Greek, but Lance told me many of the entrées were French dishes. "Just like back home in New Orleans," he said, and was actually able to translate for me. There were no prices on the menu and this frightened me, too, but I figured it was just food, so I let Lance order for both of us. The waiter hovered at our table while Lance ordered—and I thought the waiter could detect my discomfort, the way he kept smiling down at me, looking as if he was about to burst out laughing. Every time I looked up, he was staring at me and holding my eyes with his.

But as soon as he left, Lance said, "Told you."

"Told me what?"

"That guys will cream in their pants over you! Didn't you notice the waiter couldn't take his eyes off you? Don't tell me you missed that, Angel!"

"I thought he was laughing at me. I must look like I'm still wearing a straw hat and chewing on a blade of grass."

Lance laughed at that. "Quit that, Angel. The truth is, you're the most beautiful man in this entire restaurant, and they think so, too," he said, nodding across the room where our waiter and a couple more waiters were talking. They were looking in our direction, so I quickly looked away.

"They can't stop staring at you, either," Lance said, still smiling at me.

I didn't know about that, but soon enough, the waiter was back with our drinks. He fiddled with the glassware on the table, lit a candle, and centered it among the gleaming silver. I looked up at him, and he was looking at me as he continued to smile. Then, during the meal, he came back every few minutes, until I thought maybe Lance was right. But the waiter's attention only made me more nervous.

I had to watch the others in the restaurant to see how they ate, not that I didn't know about keeping one hand in my lap, unless I was using a knife and that kind of stuff. But I'd never been to a restaurant this nice. Lance seemed at home, as I say, and knew what we should do. When the waiter brought the bill, Lance glanced at it and told me how much I should leave for a tip. But when I saw the amount on the bill, my hands shook at the costs, which I tried to hide as I slid a fifty-dollar bill and some fives into the little leather notebook the waiter had left for us.

When that was over and the waiter had gone away, neither of us were quite ready to leave the table. We tried to make small talk, but looming in my mind was how quickly our trip out here had gone. This was our last night together for a long time, and I felt like crying, rather than smiling across the table at Lance. His eyes smiled back at me, above his beautiful hands, clasped together, as if this was the most natural place in the world for him to be. And I was frightened this time for myself, wondering what would become of "us," because in a way, Lance was returning to a kind of place like I imagined New Orleans to be. All through dinner, and even now as we were talking, there was a kind of twinkle in his eyes that told me he liked being here.

I couldn't help it. I had to ask. "You're glad to be here, aren't you, Lance?"

He smiled, then nodded. "In a way, Angel. Sure I am. I'm excited about living here, but that doesn't mean what you're making it out to be."

"What?" I asked, feeling my heart pound because he'd seen through my question.

"It's not going to be nearly as great as it could be, you know, if you were going to be here, too."

Still, as we went back to the lobby and later out on the street for a walk, there was a lightness in his step and a secret smile on his lips, and I knew he liked it here a great deal, and that frightened me more than anything. How could I compete for his affection with all this city had to offer—me, a hick from the middle of nowhere?

* * *

Even though we made slow, deep love in our hotel room that night, the next morning as we got dressed, ate breakfast in the hotel, and left to find the Academy of Art College, I remembered a long time-ago feeling that came over me the next morning after Lance and I had met. He was a stranger to me, then; and here in this city, he was a stranger all over again. A side of him came out that made me feel small and inadequate. I might call it his sophistication with city ways, though I'm not sure if it was that, or if I felt inadequate to this city, while he seemed to fit right in.

We found the college administration building on Montgomery Street, right downtown, and managed to get him checked in. They were expecting him, already had his room assignment at the Sutter Apartments, and an assigned roommate. I hoped the guy would be ugly, if not deformed in some unspeakable way, but I kept that to myself, and felt childish at the way my mind turned on itself, because Lance was being as loving and attentive to me as he always had been.

I could feel the time slipping away quickly, however, and it seemed like the day was racing past. We walked around the apartment building and up and down the street, looking into the shops and cafes. The apartment building had a nice lobby and common room where all the men would be eating—all of them artists, like Lance. Again, I felt inadequate. And once we moved Lance's belongings into his room, we were left trying to make small talk. It seemed to me that he was anxious to get settled in and, really, that he was a little anxious for me to leave.

I had to leave anyway, because I wanted out of the city and well down the road before I rented another room for the night.

"So…this is it, then," I said.

Lance and I were standing outside on the street in front of his apartment. My hillbilly pickup was parked a half-block away.

"I guess so, Will," he said, still with that twinkle in his eyes. I noticed he didn't say 'Angel,' and that caused a sort of 'twinkle' in my own, from the tears that burned suddenly.

"You'll write?" I asked, almost doubting that he would. I took a backward step.

"Of course I will, and I'll call you, Angel!" he said, though already his voice sounded different to me, as if he were speaking rehearsed lines.

"I...uh...better call you, to...to save you money." I took another step back, looking away, feeling a sob deep down in my chest, caught there in a wash of confusion. How could we be doing this? Yet we were. We were saying good-bye.

And then I turned fully and just waved. I couldn't speak.

"Will! What are you doing!" Lance said, sounding surprised. "Wait up for me!" And then he was beside me. He took my hand, and I thought I was going to lose it and start bawling. "Don't you even want to kiss me?" he asked.

So for a final time, right there on the street in front of passersby, I pulled him into my arms, and we kissed deeply, hungrily, not caring who might see us, and when we pulled apart, I saw that he was crying, like me.

"You will write, too, won't you, Angel?"

I could hardly see him through the blur of tears in my eyes. I nodded. "And I'll call and come visit when I can."

Then it was my turn to be sitting in the pickup, and Lance was leaning in my window, touching my face, searching my eyes with his own. "This'll be over soon, Angel. You will remember how much I love you? You won't...you know...find someone else when you're lonely?"

I looked into his eyes, too, seeing something of the familiar love, but also that distance I felt that had welled up here in this city. I held up my right hand and wiggled the ring finger. "This should ward them off."

"Mine, too," he said and stepped back. "You better get going, then, before I change my mind!"

# Sixteen
# At the Edge

The sun broke through the clouds as I was leaving and, in the rear-view mirror, I caught sight of the skyscrapers of San Francisco standing against the edge of the bay, and somewhere in the city Lance was doing whatever it was he decided to do, since he still had one more day before classes started. Then I glanced over to my right, where he had sat so many times as we drove to school together, and where he had been less than a day before when we arrived in San Francisco.

"Oh, Lance! This is crazy!" I said to the empty seat.

But he didn't answer me, and I tried to remember how his body felt against me, but it was just me, alone in the pickup, speeding along with the rest of the traffic.

I drove until mid-afternoon, passing up one gas station after another, one truck stop after another, until I had to stop or risk running out of gas.

It was sunny and cold, and I didn't know if I'd ever warm up without Lance. I filled the tank and topped it off, paid, and drove some more until after dark, backtracking our route, filling up with gas again near Bakersfield sometime after midnight, and driving right on past the motel where we had spent the night, through Barstow, then Needles as the sun came up.

I felt like I was made of rubber and finally pulled into a truck stop, filled the gas tank, and wobbled into the café and dropped into a booth, looking across at the empty seat where Lance should have been. *Crazy*, I thought, and ordered coffee and eggs, without looking up at the waitress.

I bought a thermos and had it filled with coffee and went back to the pickup and stretched out, hugging myself, falling asleep and dreaming of Lance, waking up, blinking at the bright light of day, wondering if I'd slept through the night. But I saw that the sun was falling toward the west. I returned to the same booth, ordered a hamburger from a different waitress, drank more coffee, and hit the road again.

When I drove through Kingman, Arizona, I passed the motel where the old lady had refused us a room, threw her a mental finger, and turned southeast, and continued driving, sipping on the tepid coffee from the thermos. As the sun came up and I continued driving, I felt numb, and only the pounding of my heart reminded me that I was still alive. Somewhere northwest of Phoenix under a bright, cloudless sky, I pulled in at a rest stop, where I peed behind the building, rather than going inside, looking out over the desert toward the east.

As I rounded the building, I noticed that another car had pulled to a stop and, inside, a lone man looked in my direction. I wouldn't have bothered to look at him, except I had to pass right by his window to get to my pickup.

"Hey, son," he said.

"Hey, mister," I said in return, as I passed by, barely glancing at him.

"Hold up," he said, and I stopped.

"Sorry, you need something?" I asked, looking at him fully for the first time. He was probably Daddy's age, though he looked a lot thinner, and whiter, behind his thick glasses. He had thin hair, and his forehead glistened with a sheen of oil.

"You traveling alone?" he asked, kind of smiling, though it made him look sheepish.

I didn't know what to say to that odd question. "Been traveling for most of two days," I said. "Yeah, I'm alone. Why?"

"I am, too," he said. "Alone, I mean."

I began to move off, feeling kind of strange. I didn't like the way he was looking at me.

"Wait! C'mon," he said. "Why don't you get in and talk to me for a little while?"

A light went on in my head, as fuzzy headed and tired as I was, and I gave the old man a big smile. "Sorry, mister."

"You won't have to do anything. You can just...sit here." Disappointment was evident in his face, and I felt sorry for him.

"No thanks. All right?"

He just nodded, then looked me up and down, and I moved away, feeling his eyes on me.

A moment later, I was back in the pickup and started the engine, then hit the road again. I really did feel sorry for the old man, and frightened at the thought that I'd ever end up like that. And again, I thought of Lance and tried to tell myself that the two years would pass, and we'd be back together.

But somehow, as I drove on into the rest of that day, breezing through Phoenix and catching Interstate 10, it was hard to believe we would.

# Seventeen
# *I Have to Stop Here*

There's a lot more to Will Barnett's journals. But I have decided to stop here. As I've read and transcribed them, I've seen the slightest shift in the way Will wrote. Sometimes feverishly, risking legibility, sometimes haltingly, as if one thought interrupted one he was setting down. There is a break, however, in the journals, just as there was in the first set I did about his Uncle Sean, when his uncle went away.

So there is a break here, from the time he left Lance Surfett in San Francisco and began his trip back to Hachita without him. I can only surmise that Will was too busy and probably too upset to continue for awhile.

I remember him telling me when we met in November of 2001 at the restaurant in Lordsburg where he gave me these journals that, sometimes, writing in them was the only thing that kept him sane.

I also know that moving from something familiar to a new place can throw a person off, so that it takes time to return to what has been a habit. In Will's case, he appears to have dropped his almost daily habit of writing.

But as I promised Will, I will make a promise here to continue transcribing his journals. Whether there is enough in the boxes to make three or four distinct books is difficult to say. I've rejected some of his material because it's illegible, or because it's just notes that I can't readily tie into his story. So, how many books there will eventually be depends largely on the way the material settles out in my mind as I read through them.

—Las Cruces, New Mexico, March 2002
ron@rldbooks.com
http://www.rldbooks.com

April 2022
I'm taking advantage of having total control over my writing these days, now that I am retired from an 9 to 5 job, school, or other commitments. Twenty years is a good time to reflect on just what this series of journals from Will Barnett has meant to me and also to readers. Yes, these are total works of fiction, but even to me they feel perfectly real, perfectly true as I said in the Dedication to this book. I've lost touch with most of my relatives over the past twenty or thirty years, or they have mostly passed on to the next dimension—or whatever it is.

But Will Barnett, Lance, Sean Martin, Will's family are at least as familiar to me as any of my actual relatives, and a lot closer to me, as they live in my mind. I hope this new edition attracts new readers.

—Ronald L. Donaghe, Columbus, Mississippi

www.ingramcontent.com/pod-product-compliance
Ingram Content Group UK Ltd.
Pitfield, Milton Keynes, MK11 3LW, UK
UKHW040022200726
13854UKWH00001B/308

9 798201 576073